Too Hot to Handle: More True
Stories from Madame B

Ann Summers

Too Hot to Handle: More True Stories from Madame B

EBURY
PRESS

1 3 5 7 9 10 8 6 4 2

Published in 2007 by Ebury Press, an imprint of Ebury Publishing

Ebury Publishing is a division of the Random House Group

Text written by Natalie Dye © Ebury Press 2007

The Random House Group Limited Reg. No. 954009

Addresses for companies within the Random House Group can be found at
www.randomhouse.co.uk

A CIP catalogue record for this book is available from the British Library

The Random House Group Limited supports The Forest Stewardship
Council (FSC), the leading international forest certification organisation. All
our titles that are printed on Greenpeace approved FSC certified paper carry
the FSC logo. Our paper procurement policy can be found at
www.rbooks.co.uk/environment

Printed and bound in the UK by CPI Cox and Wyman, Reading, RG1 8EX

ISBN: 9780091924966

To buy books by your favourite authors and register for offers visit
www.rbooks.co.uk

FOREWORD

Welcome to Ann Summers' latest collection of erotic tales, a new and thrilling series destined to become essential bedtime reading.

I'm really excited to be able to bring you these tales of women who boldly go wherever their desires take them. We know that our customers are the sexually confident, fabulous women who love sex and aren't afraid to show it.

From no-holds-barred stories to the gentle and romantic, I promise that this collection has something for each and every one of you. So, without any further ado, I hand you over to our narrator, the mysterious Madame B ...

Jacqueline Gold

Dear Reader,

Welcome to my latest collection of erotic stories, which will titillate, arouse, delight and, occasionally, even shock you. I'm sure most of you know me by now, but if this is your first peek into my world, allow me to introduce myself. My name is Madame B and I collect women's true sexual confessions.

Women from all walks of life have shared their hottest true-life fantasies with me and for many years now I've written them in a red leather notebook. I take it with me wherever I go, for safe-keeping, and so that I never miss an opportunity to take down a confession. Whether it's in a bar, a club, a hotel room or by letter or email, I love to hear what women really get up to, and how they push their sexual fantasies to their limit. And I'm honoured and delighted to record their confessions for your pleasure – and mine! From the soft and romantic to the shocking and hardcore, or a combination of the two, I know you're going to enjoy reading them as much I did hearing them. Some start slowly, building to an intense climax, some will have you fully aroused almost from the beginning. All of them are true. So kick back, relax, enjoy and don't forget, if you've got a confession you'd like to make, I'd love to listen.

Happy reading ...

Madame B x

UNDER OFFER

This confession is so hot that I just had to share it with you. There's nothing quite like seeing exactly who you want, and having the balls to go out and get 'em. That's precisely what this 20-something blonde did, and she was rewarded with an intense sexual thrill that was even better than her fantasies. One thing's for sure — I'll never look at estate agents in the same way again.

I'd watched those luxury riverside apartments go up brick by brick. The flat, scrubby wasteland had been completely transformed by the dramatic sweep of glass and steel. Three huge, glittering towers now dominated the skyline, each containing hundreds of apartments, every one with a gorgeous balcony — perfect for Sunday morning latte and croissants. Preferably with a fit man, of course. But then, fit men had been in pretty short supply lately.

The apartments were on my route to work, so I walked past them every day. I was a secretary at a rather stuffy, small accountancy firm; all oak panelling and clocks that ticked too loudly, and where the blokes were stereotypical spectacle-wearing nerds. Not the sort you'd go for, even after six Manhattans at the office party. Well, maybe I might. My sex life had been non-existent for some time. Only my trusty Rampant Rabbit and fantasies of Brad Pitt were keeping me going, but I had to admit they were a poor second to a real fuck.

Then I saw him. Outside the sales office of the apartment blocks one warm, late summer evening. Tall, very tall, in fact – six foot four at least – and well built with straight, dark hair that flopped sexily into his eyes. And that suit. Incredibly well-cut and expensive – we're talking Savile Row not Moss Bros. I ran my eyes up and down him, savouring what I knew, just knew, would be a toned, fit body underneath. If only guys like him worked at my place.

He was holding an estate agency clipboard, and chatting to a young couple. 'I'd be happy to show you round,' he was saying, in the poshest voice I'd heard since the time I sucked off an Oxford graduate at a party. 'We have a range of apartments here, from studio flats to four-bedroomed penthouses. I'm sure we can find one to suit you.'

So what was he doing working as an estate agent? Surely guys of his class should be swanning round their country estates, playing croquet and fantasising about fucking girls like me instead of dating dreary debutantes.

He glanced up from his clipboard and I made sure I caught his eye. Thank God I'd worn a short skirt that day. Black, mid-thigh, with black stockings and a white lacy top, just low-cut enough to reveal a tasteful glimpse of cleavage but enough to raise a few eyebrows at work. I hated my job, and the thought that I might be giving several stuffed-shirts in the office unwanted hard-ons was a minor consolation. That, and bringing myself off in the office loos at least twice a day while I imagined them doing the same, wanking themselves hard and fast over someone they'd never get. Mind you, that was no different to me flicking the bean over Brad. I was sexually frustrated, no doubt about it, and was urgently in need of a decent fuck.

He smiled. He knew I was interested, and I could tell that he liked what he saw. It was in his eyes. They were screaming I want to fuck you and doubtless my own gaze spoke volumes back. Maybe I should walk straight past, I figured. Say nothing. Make him wait. But I was too frustrated, too horny. I had to make a move right then. Why not? So I sauntered past with a smile, and said: 'Great apartments. You'll have to show me round sometime.'

'I'd love to,' he replied, the young couple beside him momentarily forgotten.

My eyes flicked down to his crotch. Was it my imagination, or did I see the beginnings of an erection? I was sure I did.

'Tomorrow, then,' I replied, looking up with a grin. 'Same time. On my way home from work. I'll meet you here. I'm Sally, by the way.'

'Adam,' he replied, reaching forwards to shake my hand.

His fingers wrapped around my hand, and I felt his middle one suddenly making rapid, circular movements against my palm. For a second, I wondered if I'd imagined it. But we caught each other's eye and the sexy smile on his face told me it was for real. I knew exactly what he was doing. This was how he planned to rub my clit.

I couldn't get home fast enough. I was soaking before I'd even opened the door. I wanted to feel him inside me, to slide my tongue right up to the tip of what I was sure would be a delicious cock, take the whole pulsating shaft in my mouth and suck him until he was screaming. Just like I'd done with that Oxford grad – my first blow job, but I'd learned fast.

I didn't wait for the bedroom. My fingers were inside my panties the moment I'd closed the front door. My clit was swollen and throbbing, demanding attention, urging me to stop teasing and rub it hard and fast until I came.

But I held back. I wanted to savour my fantasy. I slid my middle finger inside my cunt and vibrated it back and

4

forth, letting the palm of my hand rub teasingly against my clit. By now my panties were soaked, so I slid them to one side and let the juices drip down my leg. I imagined him fucking me right there in the hall, his massive erect cock rammed hard into my cunt, his balls slapping against me. I imagined him pulling out and forcing his tongue inside me, licking my juices, his fingers massaging my erect nipples, and I couldn't hold myself back any longer. My wet middle finger automatically left my cunt and pressed onto my clit, making tiny, rapid movements up and down, faster and faster, until I felt that comforting, familiar warmth spread right through my jerking body, as if every vein in my body was filled with warm liquid. I leaned back against the wall and let the waves of pleasure wash over me, my finger slowing as they gradually subsided.

'What a fuck!' I said out loud. 'I just hope he's as good in real life.'

I was up the next day at 6am, pampering myself, ready for the big night. I soaked in a warm bath, moisturised myself from head to toe, re-painted all my nails and spent at least an hour choosing my outfit. This had to be just right. The trouser suit was too manly. Red skirt too showy. A posh boy like Adam wouldn't respond to the tarty look and there was a fine line between 'classy-and-up-for-it' and 'high-class hooker'. Cross that line, and I'd be just another fuck to him. I wanted to be the best, to leave him with memories that he'd fantasise about for years to come.

It wasn't only in bed that I wanted to be the best. Just because I was stuck in a secretarial role I hated didn't mean I wasn't ambitious and competitive. The job was a stepping stone. I was the junior secretary to Maggie, the boss's PA, a middle-aged woman who wore brown corduroy suits, flat lace-ups, acted like a sergeant-major and clearly hadn't had a decent fuck in years, or possibly ever. I had nightmares about ending up like Maggie. But having that well-respected firm on my CV would hopefully open doors to a much more dynamic career, if I could just stick it out for a year or so.

Eventually I settled on a pink, knee-length straight skirt, kitten-heel slingbacks and a soft, silky white blouse, with fawn-coloured stockings. Sexy, but still feminine, rather than outright slutty. I imagined Adam running his fingers up my thighs, slipping inside my panties, and a shiver of excitement shot right through me.

At work I made the coffees as usual, all my thoughts on Adam, a million miles away from the dusty files stacked up on my desk, waiting to be copied on to my computer. I didn't know how much the apartments Adam would be showing me round actually cost, and I didn't care. Living there would be a dream come true, but there was no way I could afford one. All I wanted was Adam. Luckily Maggie was on holiday this week – fell-walking in Scotland – so there was no-one watching me too closely.

I sat at my desk, already wet, listening to the hideously slow ticking of the clock. Four-thirty. Just an hour to go. I'd take my time, make him – and me – wait that little bit longer, linger over my make-up in the office loos, resisting the urge to go into a cubicle and slip a finger into my moist pussy – never thinking for one moment that my boss was about to land a bombshell on me. He was a thin, wiry man in his 50s, with stringy grey hair and half-moon spectacles that he liked to peer over. A guy you wouldn't fuck even after twenty Manhattans. My desk was just outside his office.

'Ms Green,' he snapped, through the open door. 'Come in here. I've got something for you.'

There was absolutely nothing that man could offer me that I could possibly want... Apart from a pay rise, and I seriously doubted it was that.

'Rush job,' he went on, handing me a stack of folders without looking up. 'These will have to be entered onto the computer before you go tonight.'

'You're joking!' I blurted out. 'Sir,' I added hurriedly. 'I mean, it'll take two or three hours to input all that data and I've got a...a...a meeting tonight.'

He looked up, peering over his spectacles, his cold eyes fixed on me.

'It'll have to wait,' he snapped back, with a nasty grin. 'This is urgent. You'll have to put in for overtime. Normal rates, though.'

'B-but...' I began.

'I expect you to do this, Sally,' he snapped. 'I assume you wish to keep your job?'

It was a statement, not a question. The bully. The arrogant sod. I could tell from a glint in his eye that he savoured the sadism of threatening me unless I carried out this demands. He fancied me, he'd masturbated thinking about me, he knew he could never have me, and he hated it. I looked around the office, at the brown, dingy wall-paper, the dusty shelves full of files, at his superior smirk. I thought of Maggie, bustling about with her 'Yes-Sir-No-Sir' attitude, doing everything to please him (short of a blow job, as far as I knew), and something in me finally snapped.

'No, I don't, actually,' I retorted. 'I don't want this job and I certainly don't expect to be blackmailed. I'd rather have some girl-on-girl action with bloody Maggie than spend another minute working for you.'

He was totally speechless. For a second, so was I. The outburst had come from nowhere. All my pent-up frustra-tion – sexual and otherwise – had boiled over. But instead of feeling panic-stricken, I felt free.

'I'll clear my desk,' I snapped, turning on my kitten-heel.

'But Sally,' he began. 'I need this job done tonight…'

'Then I suggest you call a temping agency,' I replied, striding back to my desk. 'Ask for general dogsbody. That just about sums up my job description.'

Quickly, I packed my bits and pieces into a carrier bag, and marched out through the main doors without a backwards glance. It was the most liberating, fabulous feeling. I'd never fitted in there, and now I could stop trying. Tomorrow morning I'd sign on with a few agencies and start scanning ads for PA jobs at places much more lively and creative – but first there was Adam to meet.

I checked my watch. Four forty-five. Just time to slip home, dump my bags and re-do the make-up. Perfect. At six o'clock, still buzzing with my new-found freedom, brimming with confidence and horny as hell, I strolled around to the sales office as if I'd come straight from work.

Adam was inside, on the phone. I stepped through the automatic doors into an ultra-modern office, so different to the one I'd just left. Four curvy glass-and-steel desks with nothing on them but computer flatscreens, and ever-changing PowerPoint presentations projecting glamorous images of the apartment complex onto the empty white walls.

'Can I help you?' asked a sweaty-looking guy, stepping forwards.

Adam put down his phone instantly. 'Sally has an appointment,' he called across the office in that sexy, posh voice. 'With me,' he added firmly, giving the other guy a glance that would make anyone back off. 'Is it all right if I call you Sally? Please, do take a seat and I'll note down some details.'

He was just as gorgeous as I remembered, with piercing blue eyes and wearing an immaculate suit and a sexy, expensive aftershave that I couldn't place. I eased myself into the chair opposite him, allowing my skirt to ride up slightly, crossing my legs slowly so he caught a glimpse of my pink lacy panties. His eyes lingered between my legs and then flicked back to meet mine.

'Why don't I take you straight round to see one of our apartments?' he said, with a grin, standing up to reveal just the faintest hint of a bulge in his trousers, enough to let me know he was horny too. 'I think I know just what you're looking for.'

We stepped outside the office and walked across the wide, landscaped gardens towards the first gleaming tower. Our hands were inches apart and brushed gently against each other as we walked, sending a sexy shiver of anticipation right through me.

'This apartment's only been occupied for a few

months,' Adam told me, pulling a bunch of keys from his pocket. 'The owner is moving abroad. He's out in Dubai right now, in fact. It's on the tenth floor. Fabulous views. We'll need to take the lift.'

He didn't tell me how much it was, but I sensed he knew I couldn't afford it anyway. Adam used a swipe card to enter the complex and we walked up a glass corridor towards a row of lifts. He pressed the button and one of the steel lift doors opened, revealing a mirrored interior and plush carpeted floor.

'So what do you do?' asked Adam.

'I'm a PA,' I replied, stepping into the lift. What the hell, I figured, I might as well tell him. 'But I quit my job today.'

'What happened?'

'It wasn't what I wanted.'

He leaned back against the mirrored wall and ran his tongue suggestively round his lips. 'I'm guessing you're the kind of girl who knows exactly what she wants.'

The lift doors closed behind us.

'And I bet if you see exactly what you want, you go straight for it,' he added.

'You're right,' I replied, running my middle finger up his thigh, just as I'd fantasised. 'I go straight for it.'

His mouth was on mine in an instant, kissing me hard, his fingers deftly undoing my shirt buttons and massaging my breasts through my lacy bra. The feel of his fingers running over my erect nipples, circling around and under my breasts, made me wetter than I'd ever felt. I thrust my hand onto his crotch, feeling his growing erection through his trousers, the swollen head pressing hard into the top of his pants. He had a zipper fly, so it slid down easily, and in an instant my hand was on his thick, fat dick which was almost bursting out of his tight Calvin's. My clit was throbbing, longing for him to taste it.

'I want to fuck you right here,' he whispered.

The lift doors jerked open. We sprang apart, his bulging dick barely hidden behind his jacket, and my silky shirt hanging open to the waist. In front of us lay an empty, hotel-like carpeted corridor, with apartment doors running down each side.

'I can't wait,' I whispered, kissing him hard on the mouth. 'I've got to fuck you now.'

Adam grabbed my hand and led me towards the first apartment door. He unlocked it quickly and we slipped into an enormous, open-plan room with marble floors and wide, low, black leather sofas. Windows ran around most of the room, giving a panoramic view of the city.

'What if there's someone in?' I gasped.

'There won't be,' he replied, pulling me down on to one of the sofas. 'I told you, the owner's away.'

I lay on my back, on the soft, cold leather, as Adam

worked his way down from my mouth, past my nipples to my cunt. By now I didn't care how many people walked in on us. He kissed and licked his way there, pushing up my skirt to reveal my lacy suspenders and panties. Eager to taste me, he pulled my soaking thong aside and plunged his tongue into my pussy, burying his face between my legs, letting my juices slide all over him. I was so wet that I felt the dampness running down my thighs and on to the sofa, soaking my asshole ready for that thick cock. I wanted him in both my cunt and my ass – a cock that big was too good to miss.

As his nose touched my clit I let out a soft moan, and he knew what I needed. I didn't even need to say a word. He licked my clit fast and hard, sucking my juices.

'Don't come yet,' he whispered, 'I want to fuck you first.'

'Fuck me now,' I gasped. 'Fuck me now or it'll be too late.'

Adam slid down his trousers, kissing me hard on the mouth. I could taste myself on his lips and I loved it. Suddenly that huge cock was inside me up to the balls, filling me totally, the base rubbing my clit as he slammed deep into me. Adam drove into me again and again, but it wasn't enough. I pushed him off me and rolled over.

'This is where I want you,' I demanded, lifting my ass slightly. 'But first I'm going to have you in my mouth.'

Adam lay back on the sofa and I took his whole cock between my lips, flicking my tongue over the bulging head, swallowing drops of pre-cum fluid, massaging his balls with my hand. He arched his back and I knew he was so close to coming in my mouth.

'Now!' I whispered, rolling over and raising my ass in the air.

Adam plunged into me, gently at first, filling me with the most beautiful cock I'd ever had. Taking his weight on his left arm, he slid his right hand underneath me and parted my pussy lips with his fingers, probing and searching until he found my clit. Then he moved his middle finger in those fast, circular movements, just like he'd made when we shook hands, the perfect amount of pressure, our moans growing louder and louder, my juices pouring from my cunt to make my clit even wetter. Suddenly his rhythm sped up even more and I knew he was past the point of no return. I couldn't hold back any longer. My whole body began to shake with pleasure as my climax began and waves of intense warmth rushed right through me. Adam pushed his cock in hard and held it still as he came, a huge throb passing through it as he shot his hot spunk into me.

Totally satisfied, we lay spoon-like on our sides, gazing out at the panoramic view as his erection subsided. 'I think I'll check out the bathroom,' I said, standing up, picking up my handbag and pulling down my skirt, which was still round my waist. 'I can't possibly buy this flat without seeing more of it.'

'Just through there,' he said, grinning and pointing towards a door on the far left.

The marble bathroom was total luxury, though I couldn't find any girlie products, so I had to make do with expensive men's ones. I hoped Adam and I could see each other again. When I emerged, freshly made-up, Adam had poured us both a glass of wine.

'Drinks on the terrace?' he asked, sliding open a huge glass patio door. The sun was setting over the city skyline and I had to admit it was a totally beautiful sight.

'I'd love to, Adam, but I can't relax. I'm really worried the owner is going to come back.'

'He has,' said Adam. 'It's my flat. Not for sale, I'm afraid. But you're welcome to stay and check out the bedroom, if you like.'

I was speechless. 'But how can you afford this? You're an...an...'

'Estate agent?'

I blushed scarlet. 'Sorry, I didn't mean it like that. I can't even afford to buy one myself. I just wanted to...get to know you.'

'I know,' he said, smiling. 'It's okay. My father is a director of the building firm. He bought it for me.

Investment, really. And no, I don't do this with every client! You're my first. I don't know what came over me.'

I took the glass of wine and stepped out on to the terrace.

'By the way,' Adam added. 'My father's also looking for a new PA.'

Adam slid his arm around my waist and we looked at the sun setting behind the city skyscrapers, silhouetting them against the sky. And I knew, just knew, that work and play were going to be a whole lot better from now on.

FILTHY RICH

There's nothing quite like the rhythmic beat of salsa dance to put you in the mood for sex, as this woman and her boyfriend found out. But then another couple persuaded them to take their lust one step further – and took them into a millionaire's paradise where they played out their foursome fantasies. For a week, I played back her confession each night, almost wearing out the tape as I enjoyed every single steamy detail, bringing a whole new meaning to the term 'four-play'.

I've always loved to dance. Even when I was a kid, I'd put on music and really let myself go. There's something so liberating about it. When you're lost in music, really lost, you don't think about your evil boss, that unpaid credit card bill or those shoes you'd just die for. All you feel is the rhythm, taking you over completely, surging through you like an unstoppable force, as your body follows the beat. That's how it's always been for me.

As a kid I dreamed of working in a West End musical, singing and dancing every night, being with people who loved my passion as much as I did. Each time we went into town, I'd walk along the streets, staring in awe at the brightly lit theatres, with their colourful posters and sumptuous, inviting entrance halls, with their thick carpets and dark wooden staircases. And down the side streets, the understated stage doors, where the stars of the show came and went. One day, I told myself, I'll be the one coming out of the stage door, still in my thick make-up and buzzing from the show.

Did I follow my dream? Did I hell. My singing voice is pretty dreadful, to be honest, and I'm quite short and curvy – there is no diet in the world that would reduce me to Nicole Richie. Or even get me close. I did modern dance classes, and applied to a few dance schools, but at the auditions everyone was thin as a pole and wearing ballet shoes. So I decided to keep dance as a hobby, and that's when I discovered salsa.

If you've never been to a salsa class, it's hard to imagine just how incredible, how totally exhilarated, it can make you feel. The music is Latino, fast and furious, with quick steps, fast turns and lots of dramatic hair-tossing. Well, that's not compulsory, of course, but once the music takes you, it's impossible to hold back. And best of all, you dance in couples. Very, very sexy.

I'd read about salsa, so when I saw classes advertised near my home, I thought I'd give it a go. The teacher was a beautiful Cuban woman with long dark hair and beautiful coal-black eyes, who wore the most fabulous short lycra dress and strappy heeled shoes to dance in – I loved it so much that I went straight out and bought the entire outfit. My enthusiasm was totally infectious and within a month I'd persuaded three friends and my boyfriend Mike to come along and try it.

Salsa came naturally to me, but to my surprise Mike picked it up very quickly too. He's well built, not much taller than me, and fair-haired, so not the tall, slim, Latino look you'd expect in a salsa dancer. But, boy, could he move! After a few sessions we began to practise dancing together, and there was nothing I loved more than feeling Mike's sweaty body pressed up against mine as he spun me round, wrapped up in the music just as much as I was.

We quickly realised that salsa was a fabulous form of foreplay. When his arm slid around my waist and pulled me close at the start of a dance, a sexy shiver would sizzle right through me. Our bodies would be almost – but not quite – touching, which simply added to the thrill. The music would begin, that hypnotic, sensual rhythm that you just knew would be perfect to fuck to. I'd want to fuck him right then and there, and I'd know I couldn't for at least a couple of hours when the class ended. It was the anticipation, the knowing that after the class, we'd dash home, hot and sweaty, and he'd be inside me the moment we were in the front door, which drove me wild. Some nights I felt so turned on that halfway through I'd have to slip out to the loos, my fingers eager to satisfy my bulging clit, lubricating it with my juices and my sweat. Other nights I'd make myself wait, delaying my orgasm until we were home, when I'd have Mike's delicious cock inside me.

There were about 20 of us in the class, some of them couples, and right from the start I noticed one woman in particular, Claire, made a real effort to be friendly. She was a little older than me – early 30s, I'd say – and much taller and thinner, with long, straight dark hair which she always wore tied up in a high ponytail. Her face was very pretty, with beautiful chiselled features that suggested she could have been a model. Maybe she was – I didn't know anything about her, but she certainly had the face and the figure for it.

Each week when Mike and I arrived, she'd make a point of walking over to say hi. Her husband Steve was more reserved, and slightly older than Claire, but very fit. We're talking a younger George Clooney. Probably early 40s, with thick, dark hair, slightly greying around the temples which made him look quite distinguished. I'd never really fancied an older man before but there was definitely something about him.

Claire and Steve were absolutely loaded, I knew that. When we left the class each week, they stepped into a top-of-the-range, brand new convertible Porsche parked right outside. But they didn't have any airs and graces. They were also very good at salsa – far too good for our beginners' group, but whenever our teacher recommended they join advanced or at least intermediate they would insist that they couldn't make it to any other class.

One night, Mike was ill and couldn't make the class. 'Where's your boyfriend?' asked Claire, as we waited for the teacher to start.

'In bed, with a cold,' I replied. 'You know blokes. One sniffle and they insist it's full-blown flu, demanding endless cups of tea and sympathy, while the rest of us would take a paracetamol and get on with it.'

She smiled, and for the first time I noticed just how perfect her teeth were. Not just dead even, but a perfect creamy-white shade, not the bleached-white Jodie Marsh look that too many people had been trying lately.

'Why don't you dance with Steve tonight?' she suggested. 'We can share him. It's nowhere near as much fun without a partner.'

I hesitated. Surely it would spoil her night if she couldn't practise? But she insisted it was cool. 'You never know, Steve might be off one week,' she said, grinning. 'Then you can return the favour.'

She waved to Steve to come over. 'Jen's on her own tonight,' she told him. 'I've said we can share you. Is that gonna be okay?'

'That's fine with me,' he replied, smiling at me for the first time. 'But I don't think I'm as good a dancer as Mike. You'll have to be gentle with me.'

Steve took my hand and led me on to the floor. The moment his fingers closed around mine, I felt a tingle, the way you do when someone touches you for the very first time. Then he put his arm firmly around my waist, his fingers resting on the curve of my back, and we started to move.

He felt so different to Mike, much more dominant, like the male dancer should. Mike sort of took the lead, but he was often quite hesitant. Steve was the complete opposite. He knew exactly where on the dancefloor he wanted to go, when he wanted to spin me round, what moves we should go into, and I loved it. The music echoed around in my head, just like it always did, and I abandoned myself to the rhythm, letting the beat pound through my body, moving sexily beside Steve, just as I did with Mike. Even though Steve was slightly older, his body was firm and fit, and as our bodies pressed close I couldn't help imagining him spinning me round, throwing up my skirt and fucking me hard from behind. My clit throbbed, just a little, and my face flushed with both

22

the exertion from the dance and the sexy buzz between my legs.

Suddenly, a wave of guilt came over me. Salsa was sexy, everybody knew that, but it wasn't fair to start fantasising over my married dance partner. And Steve and I were dancing very sexily – I wasn't sure I'd be too keen seeing someone really go for it with Mike. I glanced over at Claire, hoping she wouldn't be furious. She was watching us intently, with a huge smile on her face. Our eyes met, and she licked her lips. And in that instant, I knew it was turning her on.

We kept on dancing, Steve's body pressed into mine, and as my leg brushed against his crotch I felt the beginnings of an erection. Thinking he'd be embarrassed, I looked away, but Steve spun me round, looked straight into my eyes, and smiled. Then he licked his lips slowly, too.

For the first time it crossed my mind that they might be swingers. I'd never tried anything like it, and until a few minutes earlier, I'd never thought I would. Not because I had anything against it, but because I couldn't imagine the circumstances ever happening, or meeting two people I found fuckable enough. But the idea of a night with Steve and Claire was making me hornier by the second.

Claire and I took it in turns to dance with Steve, and

I found myself watching them closely, turned on by the sight of them and the thought of what we could do to each other. She caught my eye a few times, and she knew what was in my mind. Claire and I exchanged a few knowing smiles.

At the end of the night we strolled outside and stopped by the Porsche.

'Maybe you'd like to come back to our place,' blurted out Claire suddenly. 'We've got a jacuzzi, a pool – it's a great place for a party.'

I knew exactly what she meant. She was making a pass. Even though we'd been flirting with our eyes all night, it was still quite a shock when she said it. And what about Mike? Maybe they weren't swingers at all. Maybe they just wanted to have a threesome?

My clit was still swollen and I guessed hers was too. All I wanted to do was get in that car and fuck both of them. I'd slept with a woman once before, at college, and I could still remember the delicious taste of her cunt. The thought of going down on Claire while Steve fucked me from behind was almost impossible to turn down.

But I thought of Mike. He'd once – in a very drunken moment – confessed that a foursome was his ultimate fantasy. I couldn't leave him out. Even though I couldn't be sure that he'd say yes, I replied: 'Sure, I'd love to. How about next week? After class? I could bring Mike…'

My voice tailed away, as blind panic took over. What if I'd misread all the signals? What if they were just being friendly? But Claire moved closer, to whisper in my ear. As she did so, she ran her fingers sideways over my skirt, brushing across my bump of pubic hair. 'Next week,' she whispered. 'I can't wait.'

❧

The week passed in a blur. But how to put Mike in the picture? If I told him about what went on the night he'd missed the class, he might think I'd been secretly fucking Claire and Steve for weeks – it was difficult to explain how it just so happened that they'd suggested it. In reality there'd been a build-up, a gradual increase in the sexual tension that meant by the time Claire suggested it, my panties were already soaked at the thought. In the end I decided to mention it during sex.

We were in bed masturbating each other gently, when I whispered: 'Did you mean what you said about a foursome?'

Mike's finger pressed on my clit even harder and in my hand, his cock stiffened even more at the thought. 'Yes,' he whispered. 'But I'd never do anything unless you wanted to.'

'I do want to,' I went on. 'You know that couple at

salsa? Claire and Steve? She's told me they're swingers.'

'Claire?' he replied, so excited that a spurt of pre-cum leaked from his swollen dick. 'The tall one? With the long hair?'

'Yes,' I whispered, my grip tightening round his cock, rubbing it faster and faster between my fingers, circling and twisting the purple tip just how he liked it. 'They've invited us back. This Friday, if you want to.'

His spunk flew out of his cock, and hit me straight in the face. I ran my finger through it and licked it off, the salty taste triggering my own orgasm.

'I'll take that as a yes, then,' I said afterwards.

&

We didn't mention it again. I think both of us were too embarrassed, and unsure if it was going to happen for real. Even on the way to the salsa class, neither of us said anything, though I'd brought myself off several times during the week at the thought.

The Porsche was already outside. Part of me had worried they'd back out, they wouldn't be here and I'd be left worked up and frustrated. But Claire bounded over as usual, all smiles, though this time she gave us both a peck on the cheek. That night Steve was far less reserved, coming straight over to say hello.

'Coming back later?' whispered Claire, her eyes shining. 'Both of you?'

I nodded. And for the next two hours Mike and I danced ourselves crazy, almost beside ourselves with arousal, at the thought of what we were going to do. Steve and Claire did the same. I noticed them watching us, their eyes drinking us in, just as we were doing back. My clit throbbed harder than ever, tempting me to masturbate myself quickly, but I knew my orgasm would be so much better if I could just hold on.

At the end of the night, smiling secretly to each other, we went out to our cars.

'Why don't you follow us?' Claire suggested, as Steve slid into the driver's seat.

'Will we be able to park?' I asked.

She laughed. 'You'll be able to do anything,' she said, climbing into the front seat.

It was an hour's drive out of town, into a wealthy suburb I'd never been to but had heard of because a lot of footballers lived there. I wondered vaguely why they travelled so far to a salsa class – there had to be one closer to home. Neither of us spoke much on the journey, too excited and too thrilled at what was to come. The houses – mansions would be a better description – were spread out along the wide, tree-lined road, each behind their own electric gates. Some were so huge and so secluded you couldn't even see them from the road.

'My God,' Mike exclaimed. 'Do you think they live round here?'

Before I could answer, the Porsche turned in towards an electric gate which opened slowly, and we followed it up a long, winding gravel drive. Suddenly the house came into view. It was simply enormous, flanked by Roman pillars and an immaculate landscaped garden complete with spot-lit marble statues and a fountain. In front of the triple garage was a Ferrari.

'Come on in!' called Claire, climbing out of the Porsche.

We crunched our way across the gravel and up the wide steps into the hallway. For the first time I began to wonder if we'd done the right thing. The house was so magnificent that I didn't feel entirely at ease, the way you do when you arrive at a hotel that's much more flash than you were expecting and wish you'd worn something smarter.

'This place is amazing,' I told her, as we all walked into a massive black-and-white marble entrance hall, with a wide staircase leading straight down into it. My salsa heels clicked on the hard floor.

'Thanks,' she replied. 'Come on, let's have a drink and a swim.'

She led us through the house, past a kitchen that was

bigger than our entire flat, to a beautiful mood-lit indoor pool, the water shimmering blue. Around us, the glass walls reflected black from the darkness outside. Steve was already there, opening a bottle of champagne. He handed me a glass and I gulped most of it down in one go.

'Let's go for a dip,' said Claire, pulling her salsa outfit over her head.

She was naked underneath, except for a tiny black lace thong, and her body was amazing – firm, tanned and slightly muscular. Mike's eyes were fixed on her breasts, much smaller than mine, but pert enough to not need a bra. There was a definite bulge in his trousers, and I felt a slight twinge of jealousy, until I told myself that her tits were turning me on too.

Could I go through with this? It was now or never. I tugged down my zip and let my dress fall to the floor.

'You won't be needing this,' Claire said gently, moving behind me and undoing my bra. I felt her breath on my neck as her lips brushed it, kissing me ever so gently as she released the straps. Now Steve's eyes were on my tits, clearly loving every second, and I felt a warm, gorgeously fluttering sensation between the legs.

'They're beautiful,' Claire said, looking down over my shoulder. 'Come on! Why don't we just dive in?'

She took another sip of champagne, placed her half-empty glass beside the pool and dived gracefully into the blue water, hardly making a splash. Beside me, Steve unbuttoned his shirt and trousers. His body was amazing for a man his age, strong and tanned, and his long, uncircumcised cock was already semi-erect, standing proudly from his thick, dark pubic hair. Steve walked to the edge of the pool, and I relished the sight of his pert, toned arse as he, too, gracefully dived in.

Unsure of what to do next, I looked at Mike for guidance. His erection was now a firm swelling clearly visible through his trousers and making me even more horny. At the far end of the pool, Claire and Steve were kissing in the water, their bodies pressed together. Mike pulled off his T-shirt and jeans, and took my hand, leading me down the pool steps.

'Whatever happens,' he said, 'this is just sex. You know how much I love you.'

We swam to the end of the pool, my naked body enveloped in the beautifully warm water, which was chest-height all the way down, my tits floating happily. Claire immediately let go of Steve and swam towards me. Without a word, she slid her wet arms around me, pulling my mouth hungrily towards her, and we kissed hard, our tits rubbing against each other. It had been so long since I'd kissed a woman, but my right hand went instinctively to those small, pert breasts, cupping them, my fingers on her erect nipples. Suddenly I felt a body behind me, a hard cock pressing into my back. I didn't know if it was Mike or Steve and I didn't care. Claire stopped kissing me and her mouth joined with whoever was behind me, kissing them hard as they forced their cock upwards into my wet pussy.

I opened my eyes and saw Steve behind Claire, thrusting hard, obviously screwing her, so I knew it was Mike fucking me from behind and kissing Claire. His hands slid either side of me and on top of mine as both of us massaged Claire's tits.

Suddenly Claire pushed backwards away from me, and I saw her and Steve in the water, fucking hard. Mike was still ramming his dick inside me as fast as he could, but his fingers were on my nipples now.

'Let's get out,' Claire said, and the two of them swam to the ladder. With Mike still fucking me, I watched Claire pull herself out of the water, the thin string of her thong wedged hard into her arse. Behind her, Steve's cock was at full height as he climbed the steps. She lay down on a huge double sunlounger beside the pool which was draped in a fluffy white towel, but Steve continued to watch Mike and me as he masturbated furiously.

'Come on, let's join them,' I told Mike. I didn't want Steve to come before I'd felt his cock inside me.

With a grunt, and a huge effort, Mike pulled out.

'Come and lay between us, baby,' Claire said to me,

indicating a space between her and Steve.

I lay down on the sunlounger and they each kissed me in turn, starting at the lips and moving down to my pussy. Mike stood at the end of the sunlounger, rubbing his darkening cock harder and rougher than I'd ever seen anyone masturbate before. When they reached my clit, Claire and Steve both licked at my crack, running their tongues over and around my bud, my juices spilling all over their faces and the white towel. Suddenly I felt only one tongue on me. Claire was still bent over, her face close to my pussy, but Mike was fucking her from behind. His eyes were closed and he was thrusting deep into her, spearing her with all his might. I watched greedily, loving the sight of Mike fucking another woman, knowing his cock had just been inside me. Now it was my turn. I wanted to give him something to watch.

My hands reached down and pulled Steve up onto his back so our mouths were touching, sharing my juices. 'I'm gonna suck your dick,' I said loudly, making sure Mike heard it. He opened his eyes and watched as my lips kissed the end of Steve's cock, running my tongue over the head and down the bulging shaft, over the huge engorged veins, as my fingers pressed into his perineum. The sight of me sucking off Steve was too much for Mike, and he gave a sudden gasp, pulled his cock out of Claire and shot an arc of spunk across the sunlounger, which landed on all of us. I knew Steve was close to orgasm too, but I wanted him inside me so badly, so I climbed on top. As Mike's erection subsided, he watched hungrily as Steve's still-erect cock speared into me and his fingers flicked against my clit.

Claire licked Mike's spunk off her arm, then positioned her knees either side of Steve's head, her cunt right over his face, so he could lick her while I fucked him. I looked down at her beautiful arse, sliding back and forth over her husband as she gasped with pleasure. She came first, her whole body convulsing on Steve's face, her pussy almost suffocating him. At that moment, he shot his spunk deep into me too, and the warm, delicious feeling triggered my own, intense orgasm, shaking my whole body harder and longer than I'd ever experienced before.

We lay beside each other on the sunlounger, listening to the lapping water, until Claire stood up and dived in, swimming down the pool towards her champagne. I followed her, Steve's cum leaving a silky trail behind me as it floated out of my pussy.

'That was amazing,' she said, smiling, as I poured myself a fresh glass of bubbly.

Steve and Mike swam down too, and we all got dressed, sipping champagne and chatting about the salsa class as if nothing had happened.

'We'd better get home,' I said, draining my glass.

Claire and Steve led us to the door, where we kissed each other goodbye on the cheek. 'See you soon,' shouted Claire as we disappeared down the drive.

My clit was already beginning to throb and I knew Mike and I would fuck again as soon as we got in the front door. Which we did. We agreed it had been an amazing, one-off experience.

The following week, Mike and I went along to the salsa class, slightly nervous about seeing Claire and Steve. But they never came back. We knew where they lived, of course, but for us it was a one-off, and I think they knew that. I'm convinced they went round different beginners' classes, looking for likely couples to swing with – and for all I know, they still are. I never knew how much fun it could be fucking friends.

BACKSTAGE PASS

We all love fantasising about sexy celebs, and most of us are happy to keep them as fantasies, never daring to dream they will actually come true. So when this lucky lady's assistant arranged for her to meet the object of her desires, she was hoping for an autograph, maybe a peck on the cheek, but this well-known rock star gave her much, much more – and she couldn't resist confessing every single sexy detail. All that remains is for you to work out who he is… And trust me, you know him…

I'd fancied him since my teens. You know the guy. I can't tell you his name, of course. That rock star. Loud, proud, and from what I'd read in the tabloids, utterly sexually insatiable. He'd slept with hundreds of gorgeous women. Possibly thousands. And in my fantasies I was one of them. I never dreamed it would happen for real.

We were sitting outside a cafe in Soho – that's me and my assistant, Sarah. Working for a large advertising agency meant life was pretty hectic, but Sarah was my rock, keeping tabs on where I was supposed to be, field-ing calls from clients whose ad campaigns weren't quite ready, and, most importantly, filling me in on the gossip. Sarah had a knack of finding out all the juicy stuff. So far she'd enlightened me on my boss's secret affair with a lady-boy, the fact my main rival at work – ice-queen Samantha – got her kicks in the loos with the stocky blond guy from accounts, and no end of celeb tittle-tattle gleaned from a friend who worked on a tabloid.

That morning, I'd signed an important new client, and Sarah and I were having a celebratory latte in our favourite coffee shop. Although she was officially my assistant, and at 22 a good ten years younger than me, we were also good friends, one of those rare relationships that worked both in the office and out. It was late autumn, a cool day with a clear, bright blue sky and a gorgeous pale-yellow sun casting long shadows on the narrow pavements. The busy London street was packed with people – everyone from casually dressed media types plugged into their BlackBerrys to lost tourists clutching their cameras and well-thumbed A-Zs.

'I need a man,' I sighed, ripping open a sugar sachet and tipping it into my coffee. 'It's been three months since I split up with Mark, and there's only so much fantasising over famous blokes that a woman can take.'

'Have you heard?' she asked, spooning the froth off

her latte. 'He's in town. Playing a gig. This Friday.'

I knew exactly who she meant. Sarah and I had spent many happy hours discussing the finer points of his toned and tanned physique, and I'd spent years imagining myself fucking him. I'd seen him live tons of times and he was awesome. There was no other word for it. Totally hypnotic. The fantasy of meeting him backstage was my ultimate thrill. My dream was for him to come offstage, sweaty, fired up and horny, to the sound of the crowd screaming for more, and fuck me right there in the wings. To fuck me hard and fast, with no foreplay, no talk, no gentle kissing or stroking. Rough and raw, that's how it had to be, while outside thousands of women screamed his name. Just the thought sent a warm buzz right through me. Subtly, I squeezed my crossed legs together, gently pressing my pussy lips together to rub against my swollen clitoris.

'I know,' I replied. 'The tickets sold out in hours. I was on holiday, remember? I spent the whole morning trying to find an internet cafe in Turkey so I could buy them online.'

'Well,' she went on, her grin wider than ever, 'guess who's got some!'

My heart went into overdrive. Tickets? For him? To see him again in the flesh, up close, for real, strutting his stuff on stage. It would fuel my fantasies for months. My clit began to throb, demanding attention, so I squeezed my legs even tighter, pushing my damp panties into my wet cunt.

Sarah reached into her bag and pulled out an envelope. 'It gets better,' she said, smiling. 'They're from a friend in the music business who owed me a favour. You have two tickets – and two backstage passes.'

'Oh my God!' I shrieked, so loudly that everyone in the cafe turned to see what on earth was going on. 'Sarah, you are a star! You've got to come with me. He's brilliant live. But I hope I don't meet him. I won't know what the hell to say.'

I took the envelope, my hands literally trembling. I'd had his posters all over my bedroom walls, and my first ever wank had been over him. Discovering the delights of orgasm in my late teens – way after I'd lost my virginity – made me a late starter, but once I'd found out exactly what my clit was for, I'd wasted no time in using it.

His popularity faded for a while (though not with me!) but now he was dominating the charts again, still single – despite a list of celeb exes – a little older, but still with that messy dark hair, those come-to-bed eyes and in-your-face attitude that did it for me every time.

'Don't worry,' said Sarah. 'The backstage pass doesn't mean you'll get to speak to him. But you should get a better close-up look at your heart-throb!'

I gestured to the waiter for the bill. 'We'd better get back to the office,' I told her, partially recovering my composure, but still unable to wipe the enormous grin off my face. 'I've got that new campaign to work on.' As I reached in my bag, my fingers brushed against my lipstick vibrator – a fabulous silent-buzzing gadget disguised as a lippy.

By the time I reached the office my panties were soaked. Thinking about him had triggered off that back-stage fantasy I'd had for years, and I knew my clit wouldn't let me rest until I satisfied it so I slipped off to the loos for a quick release. Fortunately, all the cubicles were empty, so I chose the end one and locked the door firmly. I leaned against the side wall, unzipped my jeans (dressing down was de rigueur in our office), slid them down to the floor and spread my legs as much as I could, so damp that my juices dripped out of my panties and down the inside of my thigh. My fingers slid easily into my wet cunt and I brought them up to my lips, tasting myself, relishing the moment, eager to massage my clit but loving the fact I was making myself wait. I took the lippy from my bag and twisted it to turn it on. Just feeling the vibe buzz in my hand made my clit throb harder, but first I ran the lippy round my nipples, which were stiff through my vest top. I circled each one in turn until I couldn't hold back and I had to plunge it into my pussy.

Then my fingers were on my clit, one hand holding the lippy in my cunt, and the other rubbing, pulling, massaging, bringing me closer and closer to orgasm. Each time I almost came, I tore my hand away, until the final time when I simply couldn't stop. I let out a loud moan and gave my clit what it needed so badly – the rapid buzz of the lippy. My whole body trembled and shook, and I gasped with pleasure, as more warm juices trickled down my legs. I lay back against the cubicle, sweating, exhilarated, and thinking that I'd made far too much noise.

I cleaned up my legs and my cunt with loo roll, pulled up my jeans and strode confidently out of the cubicle, straight into ice-queen Samantha, my main rival at the agency, who stood there with a wide grin on her face. She didn't say a word, but she knew damn well what I'd been up to.

'I won the Petersen account today,' I said briskly, trying to hold it together despite my red face and crumpled jeans. Why oh why had she walked in at the crucial moment?

'Congratulations,' she replied, still grinning, her voice like silk. 'I'm up for that major corporate tomorrow. If I land that, it'll bring in millions for the firm.'

I couldn't resist. Her constant one-upmanship was irritating beyond belief. 'So,' I replied, in a voice just as silky and equally dangerous. 'How is Darren in accounts?

I've heard you two are... What shall we say? "Great pals"?'

Immediately taken aback, she reddened slightly under her porcelain make-up, turned and walked away. I dried my hands, grinned, confident that she wouldn't breathe a word to anyone, and went back to my desk.

❧

We arrived at the concert over two hours before the start, but the crowds were already building. It was a short walk from the train station, and we followed the fans, young and old, towards the glittering arena. There were teenage girls in high heels and short skirts, older 30-somethings in *Desperate Housewives*-style flared jeans and floaty tops. And a few guys too, though most had either been dragged along by their other halves or were gay men for whom he'd also long been a pin-up. I'd chosen tight black drain-pipe jeans, skyscraper heels (which were killing my feet but a small price to pay for looking gorgeous) and a very tight black top with a plunging sequinned neckline. It stopped just below my breasts, exposing plenty of midriff. All those trips to the gym had paid off, and I knew I looked hot.

Sarah and I walked past endless posters of advertising my idol's latest album. Searchlights on the top of the building panned across the darkening sky, and his name was neon-lit across the entrance. There was a real buzz in the air, a sense of excitement, and there was tension, too. He hadn't toured for ages, and his fans were nervous, wanting this gig to go well.

'This way,' Sarah told me, pointing to the side. 'We go in a separate entrance.'

Backstage pass in my hand, we slipped down an alley-way, away from the crowds, and round the back to a plain-looking door – the only clue that this was the right place were two burly, black-clad security guards wearing earpieces on either side of it.

'Access all areas,' breezed Sarah, waving the laminated card on a string round her neck.

The security guard studied it closely. My heart felt like it was going to explode. I wanted to go backstage so badly, but what if Sarah's friend had got it wrong? What if these passes weren't valid? We'd look like right idiots, like groupies trying to sneak in.

'Name?' he barked, picking up a clipboard.

Sarah gave him her full name. I could hardly bear to watch as he ran his finger down the first sheet and flipped it onto the second. Halfway down, his finger stopped.

'Okay,' he grunted, standing aside and waving her through. Trying to look casual, I handed him mine. He checked it, looked up my name, and seconds later we were both in.

'I can't believe we've done it!' I whispered, as we walked up a narrow corridor. 'What do we do now?'

'Hang out,' replied Sarah confidently, marching on as if she owned the place. 'My friend – the one who got us the passes – is working here tonight. We'll find him and say hi.'

Backstage was a maze of corridors, scaffolding, wires, rooms with closed doors and people dashing about talking into headsets.

'There he is,' Sarah told me, grabbing my arm. 'My mate. Gav, Gav, over here!'

Gav came towards us, an incredibly fit guy in his late 20s, with untidy dark brown hair, cute smile and a body to die for.

'Sarah,' he said, kissing her on the lips. 'And you must be Ali. Sarah's told me all about you.'

'All good, I hope?'

'Course. I've heard you'd like to meet our main man?'

I gulped, too shocked to say a word. Sarah smirked. She'd known this all along.

'I'm one of his PR people. Actually, he's chilling in his room right now. Do you wanna come with me? Maybe we can get in for a quick meet and greet?'

I panicked. I was perhaps 60 seconds from meeting my fantasy and all I could think was: 'I can't do it.' I was wearing the wrong clothes, I hadn't re-touched my make-up, I wouldn't know what to say – every excuse in the book went through my head.

'This way, then?' asked Sarah, pushing me forwards.

'Er, yeah, great,' I stammered, my heart racing, palms sweating, and my eyes fixed on Sarah in total panic.

We followed Gav down another corridor. 'You look fab,' Sarah whispered, reading my mind. 'Just go in there and be confident, just like you are at work. He loves sassy women, apparently. We'll only have a couple of minutes, so make it count!'

Gav led us past more security to a plain, slightly grubby-looking black door with another pair of security guards each side. The door had my idol's name on it, written on a piece of A4 paper, and it made me smile. I'd expected gold lettering on a plaque.

'Wait here,' Gav told us. He knocked and said: 'It's Gav.' And a voice from behind the door replied: 'Yeah, cool, come in.'

His voice. I'd know it anywhere. Just the sound of it sent a wild, sexy shiver right through me.

I stood outside like a schoolgirl, almost hopping from foot to foot while Sarah grinned at me. Then the door opened slightly and Gav came back out. 'Come in for a couple of minutes,' he told us. 'He knows you're mates of mine. When I say thanks to him for meeting you, we've gotta leave.'

'Cool,' replied Sarah. I was too tongue-tied to speak.

'Remember,' she whispered. 'Confident!'

We followed Gav through the door.

He was sprawled on a wide sofa, tanned, dressed in jeans and a white T-shirt stretched tight over his pecs. He looked even more gorgeous in real life, if that were possible. His dark hair was longer than when I'd last seen him on TV, and even messier, which added to that 'just got out of bed' look that drove women – especially me – wild. Music magazines were scattered beside him, and he reached up to take out his iPod headphones.

'These are my mates Sarah and Ali,' Gav said.

'Hi,' he said, placing his iPod on the coffee table, those huge brown eyes fixed on mine. 'I'll shift some of these mags and you can sit down.'

My instincts told me he wanted me. There was something about the way he'd looked at me when I walked in – his gaze had lingered just a little too long. Maybe it was my imagination? Wishful thinking? My head told me not to be so bloody stupid. But there was something in his eyes – a sexy twinkle, a spark – that gave it away.

I slid onto the sofa beside him, feeling more confident by the second. He might be rich, he might be famous, he might be more fuckable than anyone I'd ever met, but sitting there beside him I realised he was human. Just another guy. And he wanted me.

We talked about his music, his tour, not once taking our eyes off each other, flirting like crazy. At first Gav was hovering, clearly ready to break off our chat if he gave the signal. But he didn't. Two minutes turned to fifteen, then half an hour. Gav and Sarah drifted off to chat on the other side of the room. Even when technicians, PAs and other bods came in to speak to him, he'd say, 'One sec, Ali,' and deal with them quickly before turning his attention back to me. Exactly where or when it would happen, I couldn't be sure. But we were going to fuck. Tonight.

I wasn't under any illusions. This would be one night, and we both knew it. He'd had a list of famous women as long as your arm, probably still having some of them. Besides, I loved my life the way it was and didn't fancy spending it under the glare of the paparazzi, holed up in hotels, hiding.

Suddenly Gav came over. 'Make-up's ready for you in ten,' he said.

'Give me fifteen,' he replied. 'Alone. You know what I'm saying, right?'

Gav nodded, and led Sarah out of the room.

He walked to the door, locked it and turned to face me, with a smile.

'Fifteen minutes?' I repeated. 'In that case, this had better be the best fifteen-minute fuck you've ever had.'

I pulled him in front of the dressing-table mirror and

knelt down, quickly unbuttoning his fly. His cock was long and rock hard.

'Suck me,' he begged. 'Please.'

I ran my tongue down the shaft and over his balls, massaging the spot near the tip, making him groan with pleasure. Then I traced every vein with the tip of my tongue before taking him deep into my mouth, sucking him hard and fast, relishing the tiny squirts of pre-cum leaking from his beautiful darkening cock. He pushed harder and faster into my throat, holding my head with his hands, helping me keep the perfect rhythm. Glancing sideways, I caught our reflection in the dressing-room mirror, which was brilliantly lit by a circle of white bulbs around it. He was watching us too. The sight of his cock going in and out of my mouth, and the look of total pleasure on his face was too much – I'd also have to satisfy myself. I forced my hand inside my tight jeans, into my soaking lace thong, and rubbed my clit, still watching us in the mirror. Suddenly, his back arched, the tip of his penis touched the back of my throat, and I knew he was past the point of no return. Hot, thick spunk shot into my mouth, spilling down my chin, as my fingers worked my clit as fast as I could. I was so close to coming, but he pulled his cock from my mouth, lifted me gently to my feet and kissed me, licking his salty cum from my lips.

'I know you haven't come, babe,' he whispered. 'I want you to hold on. Until after the gig. Can you do that for me? I want you to have your orgasm when my cock's inside you. You'll never have come like it.'

I was so close that just the merest pressure on my clit would do it. I was on the absolute edge of orgasm, closer than I'd ever been before without coming. But I knew he was right. Waiting, and watching him on stage, knowing I'd soon have his cock inside me, would blow my mind.

'Okay,' I replied, kissing him hard, easing my legs apart, trying to ignore the throbbing. 'But you'd better be good.'

He pulled up his jeans, unlocked the door and called to Gavin. 'Make sure Ali has a great view,' he told him. 'And I'd like some time with her afterwards.'

Gav was totally businesslike, but he knew exactly what we'd been doing, and what his boss meant by that last comment. 'Sure,' he replied. 'I'll get make-up in for you now. Ali, come with me. Best seat in the house, coming up.'

Sarah took one look at my flushed face and her mouth literally dropped open. We walked behind Gav to VIP seats on the right-hand side of the stage, barely listening as he chatted about the gig and the best bits to look out for.

'Did you have sex with him?' Sarah mouthed, her

eyes like saucers.

I nodded. 'And I haven't finished yet. He's invited me back afterwards.'

'You lucky sod. I'd fuck him any day.'

We took our seats just as the support band started up. 'Was he any good?' hissed Sarah over the noise.

'I'll tell you later,' I said, smiling, my pussy still dripping wet, longing for his cock and desperate for him to satisfy me.

I couldn't wait to see him on stage. The support band seemed to go on for ever. And then, at last, the lights dimmed, a familiar drumbeat started up, that old guitar riff I'd heard hundreds, maybe thousands, of times, and he appeared on a rising platform.

Everyone leapt to their feet. He looked stunning, totally hypnotic, and I couldn't believe just a short time earlier I'd had his cock in my mouth. We sang and danced our way through every well-known number, totally mesmerised by his fit, toned body as he strutted round the stage, controlling his audience, my panties getting wetter by the second. Every woman in that building – and some of the men – wanted him. They were screaming his name, drinking him in, loving every second. And I was going to fuck him.

By the time he came back on for the final encore I was so wet that I was glad I'd worn my black trousers; at least they disguised the evidence of my arousal. I squeezed my legs together, juices trickling down, the lace of my thong pressing into my clit. Suddenly Gav was at my side. 'This is the final number,' he said. 'Do you want to come with me and wait in his dressing room?' Of course I did.

Backstage was packed, and I expected the dressing room to be full of people, but it was empty. 'He won't be long,' Gav said, closing the door behind him. 'Make yourself at home.'

I looked over at the illuminated mirror – cigarettes, a chilled bottle of champagne and a couple of ready-rolled joints were waiting for him on the dressing table. Then the door opened and I saw in the mirror that he was behind me. I'd never seen anyone look so alive. He was soaked in sweat and his hair was totally wild.

He locked the door, took off his soaking T-shirt and came towards me. We didn't need to say a word. This was going to be a fast, wham-bam-thank-you-ma'am fuck, just like in my fantasies. He smelled of expensive aftershave and sweat. I slid my jeans over my arse, leaning forward onto the dressing table, then I arched my back and spread my legs so he could fuck hard and fast from behind.

'Baby,' he said, unbuttoning his fly. 'I've been waiting all night for this.'

His cock was out in a second, and he masturbated it

roughly, staring at my arse, until he was fully erect. Then he rolled on a condom and plunged straight into my pussy, still so wet from earlier that I was easily ready for him. I smelled his sweat and felt his balls slap against my arse, watching us all the time in the mirror. He leaned over my back, his fingers probing between my pussy lips until they touched my clit. I let out a soft moan.

'You've wanted this so long, haven't you, baby?' he whispered. 'I am not going to disappoint you.'

Holding his dick totally still in my cunt, he rubbed my clit with his middle finger. Desire went through my body in waves and my cunt automatically squeezed his dick. I was watching myself being fucked by one of the most famous people on earth, and it was so incredible that every single nerve in my body was alive. Thousands of people wanted to be where I was right now, and the thought made me hornier than ever. He pulled out his dick and rubbed it over my clit, masturbating himself at the same time.

That was it, I couldn't hold back. My body shuddered with the most intense orgasm I'd ever had. Now he couldn't stop himself either. He rammed his cock hard inside me, thrusting fast and hard into my cunt. I felt him come, spurting his spunk into the sheath.

He pulled out his cock, the condom full to bursting, and rolled me over, so I was lying on the dressing table. I felt the cold glass surface pressing on my skin as he kneeled down and kissed my pussy, pushing his tongue inside and licking at the juices before standing up.

'Thanks,' I said, pulling up my jeans. 'I'd better leave you to it. You must have loads of people to see.'

'You don't have to split,' he said, licking his lips. 'Hang out a while.'

But I knew he didn't mean it. And I didn't want to stick around. My fantasy had come true, and that was enough. I didn't want to fuck him again. I kissed him on the lips, relishing the taste of my pussy on them, and walked outside, where Gav and Sarah were waiting.

'Time to go, hon,' I said to Sarah, with a smile at Gav. 'Thanks ever so much, Gav. That's the best gig I've ever been to.'

Sarah and I walked to the station as I recounted every detail. She looked flushed and horny herself and I knew she was going home to wank over it. So was I. 'Snooty Samantha might be running the company's biggest campaign by tomorrow,' I said, smiling. 'But she's never fucked a celebrity.'

'Actually, she has,' Sarah confided. 'But that's another story.'

SHOPAHOLIC

Like most of us, this girl had wondered what sex with a woman would be like. Then she met a personal shopper, who had much, much more to offer than just a wardrobe clear-out à la Trinny and Susannah. Today, her personal shopper — much loved by several celebs — is the one luxury item that this rich, single girl simply cannot do without.

Saturday afternoons were my shopping day. While some of my girlfriends hit the gym, enjoyed a spa weekend, or simply stayed in bed with a fit guy and/or a hangover, shopping was my ultimate feel-good therapy. I'd get home laden with designer-label carrier bags, having blown a small fortune, but luckily working for a City bank meant I wasn't short of cash. Time, yes, but money, no. I spent my weekdays living close to the edge, putting together multi-million-pound deals for my clients, often socialising with them until late in the evenings. It was a male-dominated world of bespoke business suits, and I loved nothing better than to pamper my inner princess at the weekends and treat myself to all things pink and fluffy. I'd lost count of the number of cashmere sweaters in pastel colours and sparkly scarves I'd bought.

The trouble was that I didn't really have a great eye for style. Buying work clothes was no problem – I knew how I needed to look, with crisp blouse, dark tailored jacket and matching knee-length skirt. I went out of my way to ensure I looked utterly professional rather than outright sexy. Sure, there were times when a little flirting with clients smoothed things along. But these were hard-headed businesspeople, and I was investing their money for them. I had to stay calm, in control and confident at all times. When it came to casual clothes, I admit I was a bit clueless. So I ended up staggering home under the weight of yet another three pairs of designer jeans, various fitted jackets and a ton of strappy tops.

'What you need is a personal shopper,' insisted my friend Lisa over coffee in Starbucks one Sunday. 'Someone who can create different casual looks for you. After all, babes, you've got the figure for it.'

She was right. I'm tall and slim, but not a beanpole – I've also had the good fortune to have a decent-sized chest.

'You should try Maria,' she went on. 'She's my stylist. Honestly, darling, one session with her and you'll look and feel a million dollars.'

'I didn't even know you were styled by someone,' I confessed. 'You always look good but not in that ridiculous, over-trendy way.'

'Well, that's the whole point of a good stylist, isn't it?' Lisa admitted, with a smile. 'But listen, I don't tell everyone about Maria, she's too good to share. But I think you should give her a go. She's got several celeb clients. Trust me, you won't be disappointed.'

Lisa always looked amazing. Today she was wearing a long, hippy-chic skirt and floaty top that could so easily have looked more frump than fashionable, but there was something about the combination of colours and accessories that meant she pulled it off. Maria had to be worth a go.

Lisa gave me Maria's details and I called her mobile later that day. 'I could do next Saturday,' she suggested. 'You'll need to set aside the whole afternoon. First we'll go through your existing wardrobe, then we'll hit a few shops. Does that sound okay?'

'Sounds great,' I replied.

She was chatty and friendly on the phone, and not at all snooty, but I must admit that I had pre-conceived ideas about fashion types – all über-trendy, bit pretentious, oozing confidence. I had visions of her convincing me to bin thousands of pounds' worth of designer gear, and I hoped she wouldn't take me totally out of my comfort zone or try and dress me up like a footballer's wife. If I wasn't careful I'd end up with a tattoo on my navel. I was a bit more conservative than that. I was pretty traditional when it came to men, too. I'd had a few relationships, all long-term, and the odd one-night stand, but they were always the same – suited and booted City guys, well spoken, educated, and boring. Typically, my masturbation fantasies would be the things I'd never do in real life, like fucking one of the builders outside our office, or seducing a client. But in reality, 'play it safe' had always been my motto. Beware the unknown.

Maria arrived in a latest-model Ferrari, but she was nothing like I'd expected. She was very petite, with straight shoulder-length blonde hair, delicate features and enormous, kind-looking blue eyes. Quite beautiful. The kind of girl that guys would go crazy over. But most unexpected of all was my reaction to her.

I'd seen plenty of beautiful women before, but just one look at Maria turned me on. I felt that sudden surge of lust, that familiar tingle in my clitoris, and I knew it was Maria making me horny. Sure, I'd thought about sex with a woman, like everyone has, and wondered what it would be like, but I couldn't ever remember fantasising about it, let alone getting wet just looking at a girl. My nipples hardened and rubbed hard against my silky bra.

'Hi,' she said, with a wide, open smile. 'I'm Maria.'

Even her manner was gentle and unassuming, nothing like the in-your-face attitude that I'd dreaded. But that made me want her all the more. She seemed so soft, so vulnerable – yet I knew she had a client list as long as my arm, including some well-known celebs, so underneath that soft, easy-going manner had to be a pretty damn hard-headed businesswoman. I admired her already and even that added to the arousal.

'And I'm Zoe,' I replied, smiling back, trying to ignore the shiver of excitement that rippled through me. 'Please, come in. Can I get you a coffee?'

'That would be lovely.'

I led her into the kitchen and Zoe plonked her bag down on the marble surface. 'Fabulous place you've got,' she went on. 'Lisa tells me you work in the City.'

I chatted to her about my job and tried to stop my eyes lingering on her breasts. She was wearing tight drainpipe jeans, which fitted her slim legs perfectly and showed her pert little arse off to perfection. Her breasts were small, too, but firm – I could tell, through her white top, that she'd gone braless. She'd the sort of boobs that could get away with it and stay classy. I longed to run my finger down the nape of her long neck, over those nipples, then take her whole tit in my mouth and suck it hard. I imagined her blonde head moving up and down over my pussy as she licked my clit, flicking her tongue over and over its swollen surface as she brought me closer and closer to orgasm.

What was going on? What was I thinking? I'd never felt like this before and I wasn't sure how to handle it. Just standing there looking at her had me wetter than ever and my panties were totally soaked! I was determined to remain friendly but businesslike, confident that Maria would have no idea what was going through my head. There was absolutely nothing in her manner, or her eyes, to suggest she felt the same way. My clit was so swollen that standing up was uncomfortable, and I knew I'd have to bring myself off in the bathroom before we went out shopping.

'Tell you what,' said Maria, finishing her coffee. 'Let's go shopping first. We can sort your wardrobe later.'

'Sure,' I replied. 'I'll just nip to the loo first.'

My fingers were on my clit the moment I shut the door, and what happened next was totally overwhelming. As soon as I touched myself I came, so fast and so hard, as massive spasms of pleasure rocked my whole body. Normally it took me at least a few minutes to bring myself off. My pussy was wetter that I'd ever felt it before. Something about Maria had made me aroused in a way I'd never experienced.

Moments later, Maria and I left the flat and caught a cab into town. I'd hoped that bringing myself off would stop the fantasies about her going through my head, but it didn't. Sitting there beside her on the back seat, my panties still soaked in my juices, I looked down at her gorgeous slim legs, leading down into a pair of high-heeled strappy sandals. I looked at her long fingers, resting gently in her lap, wishing those long, carefully manicured nails were inside my cunt.

Our first stop was a small boutique, so exclusive that Maria had to knock to be let in. 'This is my new client, Zoe,' she said to the owner, a smart, middle-aged lady who offered us refreshments and generally made such a fuss of us that I realised Maria obviously brought a lot of her wealthy clients here.

'Honestly, we're fine,' Maria said, refusing yet another offer of freshly squeezed orange juice as she chose a selection of clothes from the rails. 'Zoe and I will go and try these on.'

'Of course,' the owner gushed. 'I'll be in my office if you need anything.'

Maria led the way up a cast-iron spiral staircase. I followed her, my eyes focused on her perfect peach of a bum swaying side to side with each step, my lust threatening to totally engulf me in a way I'd never felt before with a man. I didn't know how to suppress my arousal – even masturbating hadn't been enough to stop it. We went through a door into the most gorgeous fitting room

I'd ever seen with a luxurious cream carpet on the floor, mirrors on every wall, soft lighting, a cream-coloured armchair and fresh flowers in a vase on a small corner table. Even the clothes came on pink padded hangers.

Hanging up the outfits, she turned to face me. 'Would you like me to help you?' she asked, totally matter-of-fact. 'Or I can wait outside if you prefer.'

I hesitated. If I changed in front of Maria she might glimpse my wet panties and realise she'd turned me on. Then again, I decided, I was paying for her services and I really didn't have a clue which clothes went together.

'Please stay,' I replied, perhaps a little too enthusiastically. 'I really won't know what to put on.'

'No worries,' she said, and for the first time I sensed a spark between us – only fleetingly, not enough to be sure, but enough to make my clit swell again. 'Let's get you out of these clothes.'

I turned around for her to unzip my sleeveless dress. Her fingers brushed lightly over my skin and she slid down the zip a little too slowly, almost as if she was undressing me like a lover would, gently pushing the dress over my shoulders so that it slipped down to the floor. Her mouth – beautifully lipsticked and glossed in pale pink – hovered by the nape of my neck.

I looked at myself in the mirror, and liked what I saw – a very sexy, white satin matching bra and G-string set, complimenting my tan. Maria looked over my shoulder at the mirror.

'You've got a gorgeous body,' she said, her eyes fixed on my tits.

She was standing so close to me, I could feel her breath on my shoulder and the denim of her jeans brushing against my leg. For a second, we stood there awkwardly, my heart pounding, my breathing fast. Inside, I was on fire. I wanted to turn and face her, pull her face into my tits, but I couldn't be sure that was what she wanted. I'd seduced plenty of men, but how could I find out if she felt the same? Then I had an idea.

'Should I keep on my underwear?' I asked. 'Or would you prefer that I took it off?'

The question sounded so innocent, but she'd know what I meant. Or so I hoped. Now it was up to her.

'I think you'd better take it off,' she replied, her long fingers slipping inside my bra strap. 'Would you like me to help?'

I nodded, too horny to speak. Maria gently unhooked my bra and slid the straps over my shoulders, just as she'd done with the dress. My tits fell out, nipples firm and erect, as the bra hit the floor.

'Now the panties,' she said, walking round the front of me.

She knelt down, took hold of the side of the panties

and slid them down to my knees, exposing the soaked patch in the gusset. Her face was inches away from my cunt, her glossy blonde head hovering there, just as I'd fantasised. I was so turned on that I let out a gasp.

Maria ran her fingers over the wet patch and looked up at me with a sexy smile. She licked her lips, and I groaned again.

'Jesus, you're soaked. Any reason?' she asked, grinning.

I knew if she didn't touch me soon I'd have to masturbate. My whole body ached with longing.

'Just lick me,' I replied. 'Lick me. Please.'

Her face moved towards my bush, as her nose teased my clit and her tongue pressed into the groove between my pussy lips. I had never, ever been so horny in my life. She eased my thighs apart and slid her tongue deeper into my pussy, over my clit and up into my cunt.

Maria ran her tongue around the inside, sucking at my juices, before concentrating on my clit. I took hold of her blonde head and held it still as I rocked back and forth on her tongue, growing ever closer but also fighting back the waves of orgasm. Maria sensed I was about to climax and stood up, taking my whole tit in her mouth and sucking as she flicked my nipple with her tongue. Then she kissed me hard. My tongue probed inside her mouth and I tasted my own juices on her lips.

Even though she'd just made love to me, I was still nervous about touching her. I'd never been with a woman before and I didn't want to get it wrong. Maria seemed to sense my hesitation, and undid her own jeans. I pulled her top over her head and instinctively reached for those pert, tiny breasts, cupping them in my hands and running my tongue over them in ever-decreasing circles until my lips fell on her nipple. Maria let out a moan of pleasure and pulled me down onto the soft carpet, our bodies pressed together, my pubic hair bristling against her pink cotton panties. She swirled her tongue around my lips, then plunged deep into my mouth, showing just how much raw desire she felt. My fingers left her tits and worked their way down to her navel, stroking and kneading, and I slid them over the panties, now damp with her wetness. Maria spread her legs, inviting me to touch her, but I kept her waiting. I teased her, running my finger over the gusset, slipping it just inside the panties and pulling it out again. Eventually Maria couldn't take it any longer. She grabbed my hand and plunged it in inside her and for the first time ever my fingers slid inside a wet pussy.

She felt so different to me – smaller and tighter, with a clit like a tiny rosebud, but just as wet as I was. I started to masturbate her the way I do myself – thrusting my middle finger into her cunt, then pulling it out and giving her clit lots of hard, circular rubs. Maria groaned with pleasure and arched her back, so I knew she was close to coming, maybe too close to stop, so I massaged her clit as fast as I could, while my other hand instinctively went to my own, desperate to climax at the same time as her. Maria's whole body began to jerk, and as she came she plunged a finger hard into my pussy. I stifled a scream of pleasure as my orgasm engulfed me, our bodies rocking and climaxing together.

We lay back on the soft carpet, our bodies entwined. I was totally overwhelmed by the experience, but my instincts told me this was just sex for both of us – I certainly wasn't interested in a relationship and I was pretty sure Maria felt the same.

It was Maria who stood up first. 'We'd better try some of these clothes on!' she said, her face and body still flushed with pleasure. She bent down right in front of me and picked up her pink panties and jeans, giving me a tempting glimpse of her wet cunt and arsehole. Incredibly, I didn't feel awkward or embarrassed in her company. What we'd done felt so right, so natural. We didn't talk about what we'd done, but I wondered vaguely if she realised it had been my first time.

Of course, I had also engaged Maria's professional help for the day – and I was paying for it. She helped me into several different outfits, complimenting me on how great I looked. I came away with a denim skirt and pale pink blouse, mainly because Maria said I looked stunning in them. It must have been at least an hour before we made our way down to the till, but the shop owner didn't bat an eyelid.

The rest of the afternoon passed in a daze. Maria and I went to London's top boutiques and designer shops, though these were more traditional inside and didn't have a 'private' fitting room like the first one. So I changed alone, emerging to gauge Maria's opinion. By the second store I knew she was horny again, as each time I came out of the fitting room, her eyes lingered on my body in the most sensual, seductive way imaginable. I loved the way she looked at me. We were going to have sex again, and we both knew it. The waiting just added to the thrill. I even toyed with the idea of masturbating myself in the cubicle – I would have come very quickly – but I wanted to save my climax for Maria. This time, I decided, I'd be the one giving head.

By closing time I'd spent a small fortune but I had to admit that Maria knew exactly what she was talking about when it came to clothes. She'd encouraged me to try on outfits I'd normally have walked straight past – from hippy-chic skirts like Lisa's to mini-skirts – yes, mini-skirts. She showed me they don't always have to look tarty. And I'd even bought a trendy parka jacket, something I'd always wanted but didn't think I had the confidence to carry off.

'A good day's work,' said Maria as we sat in the cab home. 'Now all we need to do is clear some wardrobe space and you'll be sorted.'

'You'd better come into my bedroom then,' I said, grinning. 'If you dare!'

'I'd love to,' she replied.

Maria followed me down the hall and into my flat. I directed her towards the bedroom whilst I fetched a bottle of champagne and two glasses from the kitchen, and we drank it as she went through my wardrobe. She looked utterly irresistible, with her white top slipping slightly off her tanned shoulder, and those gorgeous, glossy pink lips just waiting to be kissed.

'That was my first time, earlier,' I confessed. 'With a woman.'

'Really?' she replied, genuinely surprised. 'It didn't feel like it. I'm honoured!'

'I just couldn't keep my hands off you,' I added, taking her champagne glass and placing it gently on the bedside table.

'Nor mine off you, babe,' she said, leaning back on the bed and unzipping her jeans. She pushed them down to her knees.

I took off my dress and slid her jeans right off, keeping my touch totally featherlight, and gently eased her legs as wide as they would go, exposing her cherry-coloured cunt and the beautiful rosebud clit I'd stroked earlier.

This time, I felt much more confident. I kissed her navel and worked down to her cunt, my lips and tongue tasting and kissing new territory. Her skin was silky soft, so unlike a man's. I had to admit I preferred giving head to her than to blokes – I never really got off sucking cock – but running my tongue around her clit, feeling it swell with every lick... This was one case where it really was as good to give as to receive.

I used the tip of my tongue to tease her, flicking it over her clit, then forcing my whole tongue into her cunt, savouring her juices. Maria writhed in pleasure and pushed down onto my tongue so it was in her as far as it would go, but I knew she wanted to be penetrated more deeply. I slid a finger inside her but still she pushed down, and I knew she needed more.

I reached into my bedside cabinet and took out my vibrator. The smooth plastic buzzed in my hand as I ran it underneath her top, circling her tits. Maria took the vibe from me, turned it on full and plunged it straight into her slit, forcing her pussy lips apart.

'Fuck me hard,' she said, curling my fingers around the vibe.

I did as she asked, ramming the vibe in and out of her cunt and making sure I ran it over her clit on each forward thrust. Maria pulled me close to her, those beautifully manicured nails pressing into my buttocks and she ran a finger over my arse and into my cunt from behind.

'My clit,' I breathed, as the throbbing between my legs became almost unbearable.

Maria knew what I needed. She ran the wet vibe between my pussy lips, her juices and mine mingling between my legs, as my fingers massaged my own tits, flicking at my nipples.

'Don't come,' she breathed. 'Not yet. I've got something you're going to love.'

She left the toy inside me and reached down into her bag beside the bed. At first, I thought it was another vibe, but then I saw a small harness attached to it. Quickly, she strapped the dildo around her waist and legs. My vibe seemed so small and pathetic in comparison. I threw it aside and opened my legs, ready to be really fucked.

Maria was on top of me in a second. She thrust the strap-on into me, sliding in effortlessly, stimulating my clit and my cunt at the same time. Her whole body was saturated in sweat and her glossy blonde hair fell over my face as she fucked me like a man. But this was better than any man I'd ever had. Her firm body and pert little tits were driving me wild. I rolled her onto her back and

climbed on top of the dildo, riding her hard and stimulating my own clit while she rammed my vibe inside her.

'I'm going to come so hard,' I gasped, as my orgasm
hit in a delicious, unstoppable wave. I just let go of all the
tension I built up delaying my orgasm and my whole
body shuddered with pleasure. I climbed off Maria and
attached the strap-on to myself, pulling the harness tight.

'And now,' I said, brimming with confidence, 'it's
your turn.'

She flipped over on to her front and the strap-on slid
into her from behind, her whole pussy tight around it.
Maria was so close that I knew it would only take a couple
of thrusts before she came. My vibe was laying on the bed,
wedged between her pussy lips and vibrating her clit at
top speed. Suddenly, Maria let out an animal-like howl
and her whole body jerked with an intense orgasm.

Just like before, we lay there entwined in each other's
arms, but this time I knew there wouldn't be a repeat
performance. You know how sometimes you get that feeling after a one-night stand? This had been an all-day
stand, the best ever. I had no idea if she was straight or
bisexual, and I didn't care. Clearly something between us
had just boiled over.

Maria began to get dressed and I put the strap-on
back in her bag.

'I almost forgot,' I said, grabbing my own handbag

off the dressing table. 'I need to pay for today.' We'd agreed £200, so I handed her the cash.

'Thanks,' she replied, pocketing it. 'Call me if you need any more shopping advice, okay? Today was fun.'

And with a peck on the cheek, she was gone.

Two days later, still glowing from the experience and looking fabulous in one of my new outfits, I bumped into Lisa. 'How did it go?' she asked. 'With Maria?'

'Great,' I replied, breezily, blushing ever-so-slightly.

Lisa gave me a knowing look. 'She's good, isn't she?' she said.

So I wasn't the only one of her clients she'd fucked. Did I care? Not on your life. A shrewd businesswoman, just as I'd suspected.

'She was amazing,' I said, beaming.

'I see her every few months,' Lisa confided. 'When I need a little, you know, confidence boost. I feel like a million dollars afterwards.'

'I know exactly what you mean,' I added, with a knowing grin, a delicious shiver going right through me at the thought of Lisa – and some of her celeb clients – being fucked with that strap-on.

Perhaps I'd been wrong; perhaps, like Lisa, I too would be seeing Maria again – for the personal shopping, maybe, but definitely for the occasional confidence boost.

EXECUTIVE DECISION

We've all got one. The ex who betrayed us. But this girl wanted revenge, and Lady Luck stepped in to make sure she got it. There's nothing quite like being in total control of a situation – or of a man who deserves no better. I admit, even I was pretty shocked at first when she confided in me. But he got off on it, and I'm sure you will, too. I did.

The wide, white, sandy beach seemed to stretch on for ever. Amanda stepped out of her luxury beachside villa, gingerly placing a bare, bronzed foot onto the sand. Yesterday the beach had been too hot to walk on, but this morning, with the red sunrise just peeking above the horizon, it was gorgeously warm. Behind her, palm trees swayed against the deliciously reddening sky. The grains felt smooth as silk against her skin as Amanda padded down to the water's edge, where milk-white foam lapped at her beautifully manicured toes.

She'd come on holiday to get away from it all, and in

Amanda's case that meant escaping from memories of him. Andrew. After a year together, she'd called it off. Admittedly, the last couple of months hadn't been great – and he'd seemed distant and unwilling in bed – but she never dreamed he was screwing his PA. Until the night when her curiosity got the better of her. Two weeks ago. Something was up, Amanda knew that, and when he'd dashed out to the off licence and accidentally left his phone on her kitchen table, she hadn't been able to resist having a look.

He'd deleted all his messages, except one. It hadn't even been opened yet. From his secretary. Trusting, loyal Lois. She'd been working for Andrew for as long as he and Amanda had been together. He ran his own small business, so the team was close-knit. Amanda didn't think there was anything to worry about where Lois was concerned. Lois was a damn good PA but she was also a pale-skinned redhead: 'So not my type,' Andrew had claimed casually on more than one occasion.

For a moment, Amanda had replaced the phone on the table, guilty that she'd suspected him, guilty that she'd even think about reading his messages. Then she'd snatched it up and hit 'read'. Her heart skipped a beat.

'Can't wait 2 fuck u 2nite,' it read. 'See u usual place & time? Love ya, L.'

There had to be a mistake, Amanda had decided. Lois

must have sent the message by accident. Andrew said she had a boyfriend. She'd be embarrassed when she realised she'd sent it to her boss and follow up with an apologetic text, surely?

But something at the back of her mind got the better of Amanda. The message had been sent at least ten minutes ago and no follow-up 'oops, not meant for you' text had turned up. She had to be sure. So she hit 'reply' and typed in:

'Cool. What r u gonna do 2 me, then?'

Then she'd paced up and down, guilty as hell, panicking like crazy, wishing she hadn't sent it. Lois would see the message was from Andrew. What if she was wrong about this? Lois would realise her mistake, and maybe apologise to him tomorrow. Or even worse, phone him right now to apologise. Or, even worse again, Lois might think he was up for it.

Suddenly there was a ping. Message received. From Lois. Amanda had hit 'read', wondering how on earth she could explain all this to Andrew. And in a split second, she'd realised she wouldn't have to.

'Gonna fuck u the way Amanda never does,' came the reply. 'Just how u like it. Your hard cock in my arse.'

She'd dropped the phone on the tiled floor, her whole body trembling with shock. How could he do this to her? Images of Andrew and Lois played in her head like a video stuck on auto repeat. Amanda sank down on the cold tiles, too shocked to cry or even to feel. She was still sitting there, numb, when Andrew arrived back home.

'Hello, darling,' he'd called. 'Just had a text from the office. I've got to pop home for half an hour. Pick up some papers for tomorrow. Bloody PA has forgotten something. Won't be long…'

His voice had tailed away as he saw Amanda on the floor, his phone beside her.

'Oh my God,' he'd whispered, snatching up his phone, his eyes scanning the last message. 'Amanda, I…'

She hadn't waited to hear what he'd got to say. 'Get out, Andrew,' she'd muttered, her teeth gritted in anger. 'Go fuck Lois. Go and enjoy her arse. And don't ever, ever call me again.'

Amanda had downed most of a bottle of vodka that night. Then, next morning, with the hangover from hell, she'd walked straight into the travel agents and put herself on the first flight to the Caribbean. She wanted Andrew – and every memory of him – out of her life for good.

So here she was, staying in a luxury villa in Antigua, an island which boasted a beach for every day of the year. The first couple of days had been tough, grovelling texts and calls that she ignored from Andrew begging her to hear him out and 'talk things over'. As if. And she'd had a fair bit of explaining to do down the phone to her boss.

But by the third day, Amanda was starting to soak up the whole laid-back Caribbean vibe. She met a few people at the bar – all of them couples, but good to chat to – and began to relax and enjoy herself. Amanda spent her days soaking up the sun by the pool, and as she rubbed the warm oil into her bronzed thighs on the fifth day she felt horny for the first time since that evening. Even the mental image of Andrew fucking Lois didn't dampen her sexy mood.

The pool area was busy, but not crowded, and Amanda was sunbathing on her front, letting the hot Caribbean sun beat down on her back, a Sea Breeze cocktail at her side. Across the pool, one of the married guys she'd met earlier was about to dive in. He was in his late 20s, posh, but with his longish blond hair and male-model looks he resembled an archetypal boy-band member. She looked at his fit, toned body, the muscular curve of his tanned legs, the soft bulge in his trunks telling her that his cock was bigger than average. Bigger than Andrew's, she smiled to herself, thinking of his long, thin dick and deciding that he'd never been much good in bed. He'd made her come every time, but he'd never really driven her wild. That was why, when he'd suggested anal, quite soon after they'd first fucked, she'd not been up for it. He just didn't turn her on enough.

This married guy was off-limits, Amanda knew that.

But surely it didn't do any harm to look. She picked up a novel and pretended to read it, occasionally peering over her Dior sunglasses to glimpse him as he dived in the pool, or, even better, as he got out. Like Daniel Craig, as 007, in those blue trunks, but even better. In fact, in her mind, boy-band man was called 'Daniel'. Each time he emerged, water droplets sliding down his oiled body, his blond hair pushed back, Amanda felt herself get just that little bit wetter.

Eventually she had to go back to the villa. When she'd first read that text on Andrew's phone, she couldn't ever imagine feeling horny again. But the last few days in the sun had restored her urges. She closed the bright blue shutters and lay down on the bed in the cool, air-conditioned room, one hand probing gently inside her bikini bottoms while the other massaged her left nipple. Outside, the sun was setting, casting its reddish glow through the gaps in the shutters, and the delicious smell of barbecue floated in on the warm breeze, bringing with it the sound of steel drums down at the bar. Amanda felt completely relaxed and chilled out.

Just then, an image of Andrew came into her head, his thin cock pushed deep into Lois's arse, and instead of ruining the moment, it made Amanda feel even hornier. She made a V-shape with her fingers and slid them either side of her swollen clit, squeezing and massaging gently until her tiny bikini bottoms were soaked. In her mind, Amanda was in a five-star hotel bedroom, naked, lying on a sumptuous sheepskin rug. Beside her, 'Daniel', too, was naked, with a full-on erection, but they weren't touching. They caressed each other with their eyes, drinking in every inch of their bronzed, tanned skin.

Amanda's fantasy filled her mind. In it, the wetness seeped from her pussy on to the rug, and she squirmed with pleasure, squeezing her clit, longing for Daniel to touch her. Anywhere. He took an ice cube from the cocktail beside him and traced it around her nipple, the freezing sensation driving her wild. A drop of melting ice slid down her tit and Daniel quickly, greedily sucked at it, before sliding the ice cube between her breasts and down over her navel, pausing to circle her navel before moving it slowly into her pubic hair.

'Rub my clit,' she breathed. 'Rub the ice on my clit.'

Daniel obeyed instantly, sliding the ice cube down between her pussy lips and straight on to her bud, vibrating it sideways with his fingers. She gasped, as melting ice mingled with her juices, and suddenly into her fantasy came Andrew. He was naked, alone, and he kneeled beside her, masturbating, or trying to, but his cock was still limp. 'Please take me back,' he begged. Everything about the scenario had Amanda in total control, and she loved it.

'Not a chance, Andrew,' she replied, as Daniel pushed the ice cube into her pussy and began to work her clit with his tongue, running it rapidly up and down her slit.

'Help me, baby,' Andrew begged, taking her hand and trying to place it on his soft cock. 'I can't come without you.'

Amanda pulled her hand away and pressed her back deep into the sheepskin rug. In reality, she was on the double bed in her villa, legs stretched wide apart, masturbating herself rougher and faster than she'd done for ages, and groaning so loud that the couple next door wondered if the single English girl had got someone in there. But in her mind she was on that sheepskin rug, with Andrew watching, helpless, as waves of orgasm crashed over her, her entire body writhing and jerking with intense pleasure. Then she rolled over onto all fours and thrust her arse towards Daniel.

'You never turned me on enough.' She smiled cruelly at Andrew, as Daniel eased his thick cock inside her.

Afterwards, Amanda was quite shocked by what she'd fantasised. She hadn't realised just how angry Andrew had made her feel, or that a hint of domination could turn her on so much. And she felt sure she'd never, ever be able to do anything like that in reality. But knowing that she could imagine herself fucking other people, moving on without Andrew, felt good. She'd had one hell of an orgasm, though she blushed scarlet the next time she saw her 'Daniel' by the pool.

By the time Amanda stepped off the plane at Gatwick, tanned, relaxed and looking fabulous, she was all set to kick-start her new life. First, she cleared out her flat and threw out anything that reminded her of Andrew, including three letters on her doormat, and deleted several answerphone messages asking her to meet so they could talk.

Next, she joined the local health club, changed her mobile number and filled her diary with girls' nights out. And last, but not least, she started scanning the papers and internet for job ads. Amanda wanted a fresh start in every area of her life. Maybe somewhere out of London, she wasn't sure. Another UK city? Or somewhere else in the world? She was up for anything. And it was while scanning those job ads late one night that she saw it.

'Urgently wanted,' it read. 'PA to managing director. Immediate start. Experience essential. Please email or fax your CV asap.' And underneath was Andrew's company logo.

Maybe he'd sacked Lois. Maybe she'd walked out. Whatever the reason, Andrew was desperate. A plan began to form in Amanda's mind. So he wanted to talk, did he? Well, she'd show him just how far she'd moved on with her life. And she'd get an apology. He owed her that.

Opening her laptop, Amanda began typing out the perfect PA's CV, with a fake name – 'Jane' – and address on it. She knew exactly what Andrew would do. He'd be so desperate – and impressed by her fake list of jobs – that he'd call her mobile straightaway. He wouldn't bother to check out her references until after an interview. Then she could put her plan into action. She wanted to take him by surprise and force him to apologise.

Next morning, Amanda faxed the CV, marked 'urgent', with a note to contact her by text as it was difficult to talk in the office. Just as she'd anticipated, her mobile beeped half an hour later. He wanted her to come in for an interview after work. Now she needed to make sure his office was empty.

'Working late,' she texted back. 'Be there 8pm. Jane.'

At 7.45pm, Amanda left her office, dressed in her best business suit – black knee-length straight skirt, waist-hugging jacket, cream silk shirt buttoned up to the neck, black stockings and skyscraper black heels. Her blonde hair was tied up in a smart chignon, a slick of liquid kohl lined her smoky grey eyes, her lips a glossy red, and her long nails perfectly painted in dark ruby.

A security guard on the main desk buzzed Andrew. 'Tell him Jane is here,' she snapped, feeling more dominant and in control by the second.

'He says go up to the fourth floor,' the security guard

replied, pointing to the lift.

Amanda jabbed the button and the elevator began to rise. A strange mixture of elation and nervousness swept over her. She wanted to end this relationship on her terms.

The lift shuddered to a halt and the doors slid open. Andrew was standing there, ready to greet her. Behind him, the entire open-plan office was deserted.

'Amanda!' he gasped. 'What are you doing here? Can you hang on a bit? I've got someone to interview.'

'I don't need to wait,' she snapped. 'I'm the one who sent you the CV. I've got a few things to say to you. In your office. Now!'

Amanda strode past him towards his glass-walled office, Andrew following meekly behind. With a sideways glance at the PA's empty desk, imagining him fucking Lois over it, she pushed open Andrew's door and sat down in his black leather chair. He stood across the desk in front of her.

'First,' she began, 'I want to tell you you're a total bastard.'

'Amanda, I…'

'I don't want to hear any of your excuses,' she snapped, drumming her red nails loudly on the glass table. Andrew shifted uncomfortably from foot to foot. 'But I do want to hear you say you're sorry. Then I can forget about us and move on with my life. Say it! Apologise!'

'I'm sorry, Amanda.'

Her eyes were level with his crotch, and to her utter surprise Amanda saw the beginnings of an erection. But what surprised her even more was her own swelling clitoris and a warm dampness on her black ribbon-tie thong. She'd never dominated anyone before, and she was loving it.

'You're pathetic,' she snapped. 'Getting a hard-on just from looking at me. Apologise again!'

'I'm sorry, Amanda,' he repeated, his cock swelling even larger.

'You want to ram that dick hard inside me, don't you?' she went on. 'Shoot your spunk into my arse.'

Andrew's erection swelled to full height, a massive bulge straining at his trousers. Automatically, he slid one hand in his pocket. Adrenaline – and lust – flooded through every vein in Amanda's body. He was getting off on her dominating him. Better still, so was she. This hadn't been part of the plan. But she couldn't stop now.

'Take that hand out!' barked Amanda. 'You were going to wank yourself off, weren't you, you prick? You do not touch yourself until I tell you to. You do not speak unless I say so.'

She stood up, her swollen clit aching for attention,

and strode round to his side of the desk, her body just inches away from him. Andrew's eyes were locked on hers, a spark of pure lust there that she'd never seen before. Silently, she undid his belt and zip so his trousers dropped to the floor, revealing his tall, thin dick straining at his boxers. He groaned with pleasure as she roughly tugged his underwear over his cock, bending down so her glossy red lips were just an inch away.

'Shut up,' she snapped in response to his moans, glancing with disdain at the engorged veins standing out on his darkening cock. Amanda took off her jacket and threw it on to the chair. Next she slowly unbuttoned her blouse and removed her bra, exposing her firm breasts and rock-hard nipples.

'Keep your hands off your dick,' she snapped, as Andrew involuntarily began to touch himself. 'You are to suck my tits, but you are not, repeat not, to wank. Do you understand?'

He nodded and lowered his head to her breasts, his mouth hungrily sucking on first one tit, then the other, looking so vulnerable with his trousers around his ankles. Amanda's clit throbbed so hard that she was close to coming right there, even without touching it – one squeeze of her legs would send her over the edge. But she didn't want to come. Not just yet. Andrew pushed his cock against her legs.

'Stand back,' she barked, pushing him off her nipple. She hitched up her skirt and leaned backwards over the desk, legs apart, exposing her cunt, the thin string of her wet black thong sliding over it.

Andrew couldn't hold back. His hand was on his cock in a split second, rubbing up and down the shaft in a frenzy, staring at Amanda's cunt.

'That's enough,' she ordered, standing up. Andrew let go of his cock with a whimper. 'You are to lie down on the floor with your hands over your head. Now!'

Taking a roll of masking tape, she taped his wrists together and wound the tape around the leg of the desk. 'Now you can't wank, you prick,' she hissed, standing over him with her black heels pressed against his shoulders. 'But you can watch someone who can.'

Amanda's skirt was still hitched around her waist, warm juices spilling from her cunt. She tugged gently first one ribbon tie, then the other, so her soaking panties fell on to his mouth. He inhaled deeply, and Amanda slid her middle finger between her pussy lips and on to her throbbing clit. Andrew groaned again, rubbing his hips side to side on the rough carpet as if waving his dick would somehow help to satisfy it.

She dropped to her knees, directly above his face, and threw the panties to one side. 'Tongue out!' she ordered. 'And keep it out.'

Licking his lips, savouring the taste of her juices from the panties, he poked his tongue out and Amanda lowered her clit on to it, rocking back and forth so his tongue flicked over her swollen bud, fast and hard. Almost beside herself with lust, but still managing to appear totally in control, she sat on his face so his tongue went deep into her cunt, and Andrew sucked her juices, tugging desperately at the tape binding his hands.

'Fuck me,' he whispered, thrusting his hips up and down in a vain attempt to satisfy his throbbing member. 'Or let me wank. Please. I can't take it.'

'Silence!' she replied, recovering her composure. 'I most certainly will not fuck you. Lick my clit, you bastard. Fast and hard.'

Andrew pulled his tongue out of her cunt and inside her pussy lips, vibrating it rapidly over her clit. This time, Amanda let herself come, but she held every muscle in her body as tight as she could, so Andrew wouldn't know that she'd climaxed. It took an incredible effort to keep still, to not abandon herself to the rush of pleasure, but by doing so her orgasm was more intense than she'd ever felt before.

As the sensation subsided, she reached forwards and ripped off the masking tape. Her knees were either side of his head, her pussy inches above it. Andrew lowered his hands but this time he didn't make a grab for his swollen dick.

'Please may I wank?' he asked meekly, looking up at her glistening cunt. 'Mistress? Please?'

'That's better. You are now addressing me correctly.' She stood up, still with her legs either side of his head, the stems of her black heels pressing into his cheeks. Relishing every moment, she stepped over him, the heel of her stiletto brushing over his lips. 'You may wank but you may not spunk up until I say so. Understood?'

'Yes, mistress,' he replied.

She knew he wouldn't be able to hold back, but watching him try gave Amanda such a thrill. His hand grasped his pulsating cock, trying to masturbate it slowly, speeding up every few seconds until he forced himself to slow his rhythm.

'Please let me come, mistress,' he begged, spurts of pre-cum leaking out of his desperate dick. But before she could reply, he gasped and a massive stream of shiny spunk shot out of the end of his cock so fast that it landed on his cheek, dripping down towards his neck.

'I did not give you permission to ejaculate,' she snapped. 'Your punishment is to swallow it.'

Amanda bent down and ran her finger through it, feeding the cum into his mouth. Andrew licked his lips, savouring the taste of himself. Then she stood up, her ribbon-tie panties in her hand, and smoothed down her skirt.

'Will I see you again?' Andrew asked. She looked down at him, so feeble there with his limp cock dribbling on his thigh and his trousers still around his ankles.

'No,' she replied. 'You screwed things up, Andrew. All by yourself. By fucking Lois. But at least now I can be totally sure that you know exactly what you're missing. I've just fucked you the way she never did.'

She turned on her black skyscraper heel, picked up her jacket and walked to the lift, stuffing her soaked panties in her handbag, feeling on top of the world as she knew she was leaving Andrew behind her for good.

'Goodnight, madam,' said the security guard, as she strode past. 'Have a fabulous evening.'

'Thanks,' Amanda replied with a smile, stepping out into the rain-washed street and ready to start her new life. 'I certainly will.'

TUNNEL VISION

Have you ever boarded a train and been lucky enough to find that fate has sat you across from the most desirable man on the planet? This gorgeous brunette has – and was ready to take total advantage of the situation on the Eurostar from London to Paris. After all, what better way to make time fly on a long journey... Ask yourself, if you were on that train, would you have been able to say no?

My luck was in the day my sister Julia moved to Paris. I loved the city, with its arty Latin Quarter, crazy drivers and ever-present aroma of coffee, croissants and Gauloises. Now I had an excuse to visit as often as I liked, and a gorgeous apartment to stay in for free, overlooking the rooftops of Montmartre.

She'd landed a job at a French art gallery, and was now hooked up with the most gorgeous Frenchman imaginable. I know you shouldn't fantasise over your sister's man but with her boyfriend, Claude, it was impossible not to. He had shoulder-length, very dark, hair, amazing green eyes and an amazingly toned bod. When I joined them on holiday in Nice once, I spent the entire two weeks trying not to lust after him.

I'd never have done anything, of course. But it did mean that I felt pretty damn sexually charged when I was staying with them. Unfortunately none of Claude's friends fitted the bill. Most were hooked up with beautiful Parisian girls, who seemed able to throw on a pencil skirt, cashmere cardie and sunglasses, and look totally Audrey Hepburn without even trying.

I usually stayed with Julia for a weekend every couple of months. My routine was always the same – take the Friday off, catch an early-morning Eurostar to Paris. Soak up my hangover with buffet-car coffee and a baguette. By the time we pulled into the Gare Du Nord, I was revived and ready to step out into the busy Paris streets, past the newspaper kiosks laden with papers and magazines, past the restaurants setting up for lunch and the delicious smell of garlic and wine, up the hill to the cobbled, quaint streets of Montmartre, with the giant white church of the Sacré Coeur perched on the top like a wedding cake.

Julia's apartment was down a small side-street, close to Montmartre's central square, where, day and night, artists would sit and draw portraits for the thousands of tourists. I'd slip inside – she'd given me a key – and take a long, sensual shower in their luxurious walk-in wet-room before meeting Julia for lunch near the art gallery where she worked. It was a trip I'd made so many times that there was no reason to think today would be any different.

The Eurostar entrance hall was absolutely packed with businesspeople, mainly men smartly dressed in suits and ties. By contrast, I looked quite casual, in my pink vest and summery skirt, though still sexy, of course! My make-up was light and fresh, with a slick of clear gloss on my lips. I'd learned the secret of successful travel – look good but be comfortable. When everyone else stepped off in Paris, sweaty and crumpled, I'd look as sexy and fresh as I did when I got on.

I shoved my ticket in the automatic reader and made my way to the security check. There was a huge delay, so we had to wait in line, and that's when I saw him. He was lifting his briefcase on to the X-ray conveyor belt opposite me. Talk about gorgeous. Tall, broad, with short, mid-brown hair and male-model looks. My eyes lingered just a second too long, because in that second he turned to walk past the X-ray machine and saw me staring at him.

My instinct was to look away, embarrassed. But I didn't. I held his gaze briefly, and smiled. He smiled back. Perfectly even, white teeth, just like a toothpaste ad. For a moment I wondered if he really was a model, but dismissed it instantly – he was dressed in a business suit.

In that split second of eye contact we told each other all we needed to know. We wanted each other. It didn't matter that it was 8am, that we were in a crowded station, or even that I'd had a fabulous orgasm just two hours earlier courtesy of my Rampant Rabbit.

'Madam!' snapped a voice beside me. 'Luggage on the conveyor belt. Please.'

I dumped my rucksack on the belt, and tried to shake all thoughts of him from my mind. The chances of us being on the same train were incredibly slim – there were masses of departures on the boards for Paris, Lille, Brussels, Disneyland. And even if we were, the Eurostar trains were so huge that we wouldn't see each other anyway. I promised myself that if I did see him again, I'd give him my number.

A long travelator took me up to the platforms, and I climbed on board my carriage, relieved to see it was right next to the buffet car. Mine was a forward-facing window seat, one of a group of four with a table in the middle.

The train began to fill up, and a French couple took the two aisle seats, but still the seat opposite me was empty. I buried my head in a book, just as I did on any public transport, so that fellow travellers got the message I wasn't interested in hearing their life stories. Suddenly, I heard a deep, well-spoken voice say: 'Excuse me, that's my seat.'

I looked up. He was standing in the aisle, holding his ticket, six foot of pure, unadulterated, object of lust! The French lady looked up, puzzled, so he repeated it in perfect French, sounding deeply sexy, apologising that he'd addressed her in English. Impressed, she stood up and he slid past her into the seat opposite me, giving me a quick smile as he did so. Then he smoothed out a copy of *Le Monde* and started reading.

I buried myself in my book but my pulse was racing. There was something about him – whether it was his looks, his confidence, or a combination of the two, I couldn't be sure – that made me hornier than I'd felt in years. And I'd be sitting opposite him for almost three hours. He looked up briefly, his eyes lingering on my glossy lips, and I was sure my slightly reddening cheeks gave the game away.

The train jolted out of the station, only partly full, so the French couple moved to some spare seats further down the carriage. There was no-one seated near us. For the next few minutes I pretended to read my book, occasionally glimpsing him over the top of it, taking in that perfect, chiselled face, those huge, broad shoulders, and imagining his tanned pecs, firm and hard, and his cock, tall and erect, under that suit. Just thinking about him aroused me, and each time I squeezed my thighs together, trying to satisfy my engorged clit, my panties felt that little bit damper. My nipples were poking, rock-hard, through my vest, so all I could do was rest my arms over them and hope he didn't notice.

I wanted to fuck him so badly, but we hadn't even spoken. And I was sure he felt the same. Each time we caught each other's eye, there was an intense sexual, animal attraction that didn't need words. I had to give him my number, that was for sure. Fuck him standing up in that walk-in shower room, the warm water running down our bodies as he thrust deep inside me. I closed my eyes for a moment, lost in my fantasy, crossing my legs to squeeze my throbbing bud. As I did so, my leg accidentally brushed against his.

'Sorry!' I said automatically.

'No problem,' he replied, with a smile, climbing out of his seat. 'I'm going to the buffet car. Can I get you a coffee?'

'Thanks,' I replied. 'Black, no sugar.'

'By the way, I've just found this on the floor,' he went on, handing me a business card. 'Did you drop it?'

I took the card. 'No, it's not mine,' I replied, puzzled. 'It's a man's name. Look.' I turned the card round to show him. 'Business development manager.' There were numbers in Paris and London, and a mobile.

'So sorry,' he said, his eyes sweeping over me suggestively. 'My mistake. That's one of my cards. I must have dropped it when I sat down.'

He walked off towards the buffet car, leaving the card in my hand. 'Black, no sugar, coming right up.'

My heart raced. He'd given me his number! All I had to do was chat to him for the rest of the journey and arrange to meet up sometime. We'd fuck for sure, maybe in Paris, maybe in London. The chemistry between us couldn't be ignored. But I couldn't wait. I wanted that cock inside me right now, right here, on this train. My cunt was soaked, my clit was on fire, my cotton panties were drenched. I didn't want it to go to waste.

As soon as he was out of sight, I pulled out my phone. Could I risk it? Could I send him a sexy text? Was that why he'd given me his number?

My hands shaking with lust, I switched my phone to 'silent' mode and hit the button for 'new message'. What should I write? I needed to send it before he came back. So I tapped in: 'I'm wet just looking at you,' and hit 'send'.

The moment I sent it, I regretted it. What if he thought I was some kind of weirdo? What if he didn't fancy me at all and was just being friendly? So I laid my phone on my lap, picked up my book and acted as if nothing had happened.

He came back with the coffees and an enormous grin on his face. 'Here you go,' he said, sliding back into his seat, his green eyes sparkling with lust behind their black lashes.

'Thanks,' I said coldly, my attention fixed on my book. Across the table, I glimpsed him texting. Seconds later, my phone vibrated silently in my lap. It was resting on top of my pussy, the bottom of it just an inch or two away from my clit, and the vibrations sent a sexy buzz right through it, bringing me so close to orgasm that I could have brought myself off there and then.

Wait, I told myself. Don't make a grab for your phone. He's only guessing it's you. A minute ticked past, maybe two, as I used all my energies to keep my composure and ignore the quivering bud between my legs. I glimpsed him texting again. This time, I looked down at my phone.

There were two messages. As casually as I could, I pressed 'read'.

'Would you like me to do something about it, gorgeous?' was the first reply.

Then came the second:

'I could lick your clit until you come. Right here, right now. Just give me the nod.'

I looked across at him and nodded, almost imperceptibly. But it was enough. Without a word, he slid under the table. Trembling with anticipation, I eased myself right back in my seat, so my pussy was resting on the edge of it. My silky skirt fell over my knees, providing the perfect cover.

I felt his warm breath between my legs as he ran his tongue over the gusset of my panties, breathing hard. He slid the panties to one side and held them there as he worked my clit with his tongue, licking it slowly up and down, as my big, hard nipples pressed into my vest. There was no-one in sight, so I slid my right hand under my vest and rubbed my nipple fast, the same way I wanked my clit, so horny that I didn't care if anyone saw us, but getting off on the fact that someone just might. His tongue made slow, circular movements over my clit before plunging into my pussy, his mouth sucking at my juices as they spilled down his face and onto the rough seat.

Moving closer and closer to orgasm, I thrust my hips up and down, trying to speed up his licking to match my desires. But as quickly as he'd started, he stopped. Silently, he emerged from under the table, leaving me on the verge of the wildest orgasm I'd ever had. He gently wiped his mouth on a napkin and picked up his newspaper and sipped his coffee as if nothing had happened.

For a moment, I thought he'd misjudged it. Maybe my rocking made him think I'd come. But when I caught his eye, he licked his lips, and I knew exactly what he was doing. He wanted to tease me, taking me right to the edge and then stopping, so that when I did come it would be the most incredible, intense orgasm of my life.

Two can play at that game, I decided, resisting the urge to finish myself off with just a few strokes of my finger. I slid under the table and unzipped his trousers underneath his newspaper, revealing a long, thick, circumcised cock, the head pulsating with desire. Before I could take him in my mouth, his hand was around it in an instant, stroking it up and down, pre-cum leaking with almost every wank, and his fist banging against the underneath of the table. I forced his fingers off his dick – like me, he too was so close to coming that he couldn't control himself, so it was up to me to do it for him. Holding his hands away, I lowered my mouth over his cock, letting it press into the back of my throat, sucking as much of the shaft as I could take. He let out an involuntary groan as I moved my hand up and down his penis, soft and slow, and cupped his balls in my hand. Like me, he was on the verge of orgasm, and like me, he was going to have to wait. I gave his cock several more long, slow sucks, then flicked my tongue over the head, savouring the pre-cum before sliding back into my seat.

I took a sip of my coffee and we grinned at each other, our bodies rocking gently with the train, the intensity between my legs and, I imagined, his, almost unbearable. His hands went down to his cock and I thought he was going to masturbate to orgasm right there in front of me, but instead he forced it back inside his trousers and zipped them up.

'I'm going to the loo,' he said. 'If you're not there in two minutes it'll be too late.'

I knew what he meant. The bulge in his trousers was absolutely enormous, so huge that he had to do up his jacket to try and cover it. My own clit was swollen, the edge of my panties rubbing it every time I moved, sending waves of pleasure through me. But it was the waiting that made this fuck so horny.

'I'll be there in five,' I said. 'Believe me, it'll be worth waiting for.'

I don't know how I managed to stay there for five minutes. Just the thought of him in that cubicle, yanking at his dick and then forcing himself to stop, drove me totally wild. But I sat there, staring at my flushed reflection in the window, ignoring the flat French fields that flashed past outside as we sped towards Paris.

I waited five minutes, then ten, hoping I hadn't misjudged it and he'd shot his load too soon. He didn't come back. Smoothing down my skirt, I sauntered up the carriage, past several other passengers, through the sliding door to the toilets. To my total horror, a woman passenger was standing outside.

'Been in there ages,' she grumbled.

'My, er, husband,' I replied. 'He gets travel sick.' I

rapped on the door. 'Darling,' I called. 'Are you all right?'

The door opened a few inches. 'You'd better use another loo,' I told her. 'I'll go and see how he is.'

She turned and walked away as I slipped inside.

He was naked from the waist down, his hard, erect cock looking fat and delicious as it curved upwards out of his pubic hair. 'I almost came,' he whispered, as we kissed hard. 'I don't know how I stopped myself.'

'I'm glad you did,' I breathed, turning round and bending over the sink, feeling the metal cold against my arms, my skirt falling forwards so my soaking pussy and arse were in the air. 'Because I want your cock inside me.'

He teased me for a moment, resting his cock at the entrance of my pussy, pushing the head in just an inch, when I wanted his whole cock to fill me up. It was hard to keep my balance as the train rocked, so I held on to the metal taps with one hand, while the other instinctively went down to my clit, my fingers circling it as I tried to push my pussy backwards on to his cock. Each time I did, he moved back a little, so only an inch of his cock was inside me. 'Fuck me hard,' I begged. 'Please. Don't tease me.'

I didn't have to ask twice. Suddenly he thrust his giant, rock-solid cock forwards, deep inside, filling me completely as he pounded over and over again, spearing me harder and faster than ever, following the rhythm of the rocking train. But it wasn't enough. I wanted him in my arse too.

'Both ways,' I begged, my fingers frantically working my clit. 'Fuck me both ways.'

He knew what I meant. My slippery juices meant my arse was already lubed up and ready for him. He pressed into my arsehole, gently at first, then began fucking me hard, just like I'd begged him to, while his hands reached for my tits and fingered my nipples. Then he pulled out of my arse and plunged back into my cunt, a pattern he repeated over and over – making my whole body shiver and tingle as hot waves of desire flooded through it. No-one, but no-one, had ever fucked me like that. He knew I was going to come, so he plunged deep in my arse and vibrated his fingers over my clit. It was too much. I shook from head to toe with the most immense orgasm I'd ever experienced, and as I did so he came too, shooting his spunk inside me.

Thoroughly satisfied and exhausted, we stayed there for a few minutes, bent over the sink, our bodies pressed together as his cock softened and went limp, rocking gently in time with the train. Eventually we broke apart and stood up. He retrieved his trousers from the coat hook on the back of the door, zipped them up, kissed me gently on the nose and slipped out of the cubicle, leaving me to freshen up.

When I got back to my seat, he'd gone. I wasn't surprised. I knew he was somewhere on the train, but I had to admit it would have been awkward making conversation after what we'd just done. There was still a good hour and a half to go. But on my seat was the business card he'd given me earlier, with the words 'call me' and a kiss written on it. I slipped it into my bag and settled back in my seat, totally at peace with the world. I could decide later whether to call.

I looked around as everyone poured off the train and into the Gare Du Nord, hoping to catch his eye, but I didn't see him. By the time I reached Julia's place, after a hot, sticky walk through Montmartre, I was ready for a shower. But before I could turn on the taps, my mobile rang.

'That was incredible,' he said. 'I just wanted you to know that I've never done anything like that before.'

'Nor have I,' I replied.

'Can I see you again?' he asked. 'Maybe dinner? Tonight?'

'I've got a better idea,' I said, looking at Julia's inviting wet-room... I could always text her and say I couldn't make it for lunch. 'Come round now. I'm about to have a shower so we could have it together…'

'Give me your address,' he replied. 'I'm on my way.'

DOUBLE FANTASY

I'm pretty unshockable when it comes to hearing people's confessions. But what these naughty twins got up to surprised even me. They shared everything — even their men. Not in an incestuous way, of course, but they made sure that if a guy was fabulous in bed, they both got to try him for size...

My identical twin sister Annie and I have always been close. Not surprising, really, when you think we were born just three minutes apart. I was first, and even though we look absolutely identical in every way — from our long auburn hair to our thickly lashed green eyes, hourglass curves and very, very long legs — our characters are a little different. I'm much more in-your-face, pushy, and if I see something — or someone — I want, I go straight for it. Annie's a touch more laid-back, slightly shyer, more will- ing to let the world pass by and see what comes her way. As kids, I'd be the one daring Annie to try new things, and as we became teenagers the pattern continued — I'd talk her into wearing that incredibly sexy dress, or calling the latest fit man she'd spotted.

We'd always shared everything – what's mine was hers, and vice-versa. It didn't matter if it was hairbrushes, make-up, CDs, clothes, a flat, and later on, men. Yes, we even shared our men. Quite shocking, I guess, when you first hear our tale. Not all our men, of course, just the ones who were a really good fuck. If either of us dated someone who was fun, fabulous in bed but definitely not relationship material, then we made sure that the other got a piece of the action.

It all started by accident. We didn't deliberately set out to sleep with the same men, though we always fancied the same types – tall, dark-haired hunks with a hint of stubble, basically anyone who looked like Matthew Fox from *Lost*. But for a time when we were flatmates, my sister started dating this gorgeous builder, Danny. I'd never met him, but Annie had shown me a picture and in it he had a body to die for – muscular, tanned, with a sheen of sweat on the surface, as if he'd got a thin layer of body oil over him (maybe he had!). She'd met him after walking past a building site and he'd wolf-whistled. Being Annie, she'd blushed and walked straight past. But the next day he'd asked her out, and after much persuasion from me that night, she'd said yes. It was a pretty casual hook-up; he didn't exactly challenge her intellectually. The sex, however, or so she told me, was amazing. 'He's got this thing he does to you, Debbie,' she gushed. 'I wish you could try it.'

I didn't think any more about it, until a few weeks later when Annie came dashing in to our flat from work, her face alive with happiness. 'That guy at work, Mike, he's finally asked me out!' she exclaimed. I was so happy for her. She'd adored Mike from afar for at least six months.

'You lucky cow,' I joked. 'I haven't had a decent shag for months and you've got them queueing up! Better give Danny the boot. Unless you want to keep him on the side for sex.'

'Of course not!' laughed Annie. 'Poor Danny, though... I'm gonna ring him now. We're supposed to be going out tonight.'

The thought struck us both at the same moment, just like our thoughts often did. We looked at each other and giggled. There was no need to say what was on our minds – we knew.

'Do you think we'd get away with it?' I asked.

'Why not?' replied Annie, clearly buoyed up from her chat with Mike and displaying a new-found, go-getting confidence. 'Danny and I don't do much talking. It's a quick glass of wine in his flat and straight to bed. You could find out what he's like.'

I hesitated. Danny had never actually seen me, and

sure, Annie and me are the absolute image of each other, but what if he could just somehow tell that I wasn't actually his girlfriend?

'Danny? Not exactly Mr Intuition, Debs,' went on Annie. 'Besides, he won't even care. Look, if he fancies me, he'll obviously fancy you,' she replied. 'We're completely identical. He knows I live with my sister but I don't think I even mentioned we're twins. And even if I did, I doubt he'd remember.'

Three months without sex – and the prospect of a night with Danny – was too much to turn down. Annie gave me the full briefing – living room straight ahead, bedroom on the right. Bathroom down the corridor. Talk about work – mainly his – to avoid giving anything away. So two hours later, nervous as hell, wearing Annie's favourite knee-length silky skirt with a devilishly sexy, silky black bra and panties underneath, I found myself on Danny's doorstep. He lived in a flat on a rough side of town, where even the doorbell looked so ingrained with dirt you didn't want to push it. I'd just begun to think it was a bad idea and was thinking about going back home when Danny opened the door. He was barefoot, wearing a sleeveless vest and jeans, and looked absolutely gorgeous.

'Annie!' He smiled, pulling me roughly towards him and kissing me hard. 'I saw you coming up the path.'

Being kissed full-on by a total stranger – albeit a gorgeous one – came as a bit of a shock, and without thinking, I instinctively pulled back. 'Are you okay, babe?' he asked, genuine concern in those huge brown eyes.

'Sure,' I replied breezily. 'Sorry, I had a tough day at work. Be all right in a minute.'

I followed him in to the living room, which fortunately was clean and tidy, and sat on the sofa. Danny poured me a glass of wine and opened himself a beer. 'I know what'll take your mind off work,' he said, crouching down between my legs and licking his lips.

He slid his rough, thick hands under my thighs and up my skirt, kneading my flesh gently. My heart pounded with a combination of panic and desire. An incredibly sexy stranger was about to plunge his face into my cunt. I could make an excuse and leave, or I could lie back, close my eyes and enjoy it. Needless to say, I did the latter.

Danny's expert fingers massaged their way up my thighs towards my aching cunt, getting closer and closer until I could feel his warm, beery breath through my black silky panties. I ran my own fingers over his gorgeously muscular arms, savouring every inch of warm, moist flesh, every vein, the thrill making me realise that I really hadn't had sex for a very long time. He pushed my skirt up over my hips, revealing my legs and pussy, as beads of sweat slid over my tits, one drop passing over my

107

right nipple, sending a sudden, sexy chill through my nipple and my clit. There was no stopping now. I eased my legs wide apart, inviting Danny to leave my thighs and concentrate on my swollen, throbbing bud, just a couple of centimetres away from his wet lips. Danny knew what I wanted and deftly slid aside my soaked gusset, opening my engorged pussy lips with both hands, allowing cool air to waft over my bright red bud. He plunged a finger deep inside me while my own fingers circled my hard nipples. Having huge tits meant I could cup one in both hands and hold it up to my mouth, sucking hard and flicking it with my tongue.

'I didn't know you could do that,' gasped Danny, looking up from between my legs, relishing the sight of me sucking at my tit. I let go with one hand and pushed his head back where I needed it – between my legs.

'Gosh, Annie, aren't you the little dominatrix today?' He smiled – and this time he began rubbing my clit with his nose while forcing his tongue quickly in and out of my swollen pussy, working it closer and closer to orgasm. I watched his head bobbing faster and faster between my legs and his own right hand tugging furiously underneath his crouched body, presumably wanking his cock. Desperate to see it, I lifted up both stilettoed feet, rested them on his shoulders and pushed him backwards on to the floor.

Danny's dick was poking out of his flies, pretty small by most standards, and I wondered what satisfaction Annie got from it – obviously enough to claim he was a really great fuck – but after three months of no sex I didn't care. It was fully erect, darkening by the second, and just what I needed to fill the aching void. His whole face turned purple as he looked up at me, fighting the urge to come, standing with one leg either side of his chest, rubbing my own clit in soft, gentle circles. I kneeled down and lowered myself up and down on his dick, so wet by now that I could barely feel it. His hips lifted off the carpet as he thrust inside me.

'Do you want it?' asked Danny, slowly massaging my arsehole with his finger. I didn't know exactly what he meant, but had a pretty good idea.

Now it was his turn to take the lead. He rolled me on to my stomach, pulled off my panties and slid a finger into my arse, well lubed with pussy juice, confirming my suspicion. His cock might not be big enough to properly satisfy my cunt, and he knew it, but it would fill my arsehole. This was virgin territory; clearly there were some things that Annie had done before me! I raised my bottom up, and braced myself for a moment of searing pain as his cock plunged into it.

'God, you're so tight today,' he breathed, thrusting into my arse with all his might. 'So tight. It's fabulous.'

He was right. It felt sensational. Our bodies were pressed together, with Danny on top, but he took most of his bodyweight with his left arm while frantically flicking my clit with his right hand. His cock fitted inside me perfectly, giving me an exquisite sensation I'd never felt before. There was no way I could stop myself coming now. The intense feeling built up and up until it exploded right through my body, causing my arsehole to grip on to his cock tighter than ever. Danny shot his spunk instantly, his cock as hard as a rod, filling me up with his warm, wet cum. I felt totally satisfied, dizzy with the release of tension and pleasure that completely overwhelmed me. Annie had been right – this was one fuck I really didn't want to miss. We lay together for a few moments, until he rolled off and took a swig of his beer.

'I'll take a shower, if that's okay,' I said, smoothing down my skirt and picking up my panties. 'Then I've got to get back.'

'Sure,' he replied, kissing me on the nose. 'You seem different today. More bossy.'

'It's just work,' I replied casually. 'Tough day, you know. Made me a bit, er, aggressive.'

'Well,' he continued. 'I like it. And that thing you did, making your arse so tight, I don't know how you did it, but it was mind-blowing. Like you'd never been fucked that way before.'

I grinned. 'Oh, er, just a little trick of mine.' Not exactly surprising, seeing as it was my first time. Shame I couldn't tell him that... He might be flattered, but Annie and I would be found out.

'Maybe I'll see you Friday?' he added.

'Maybe,' I said, smiling.

Annie couldn't wait to hear all about it when she got back from her date with Mike. 'Well... I got to sample Danny's speciality.' I grinned. 'Something I guess you're much more experienced at?'

She blushed. 'I've never told you how much I love anal sex,' she confessed. 'Are you going back for more?'

I did. Several times over the next couple of weeks. And he never guessed. So after that, whenever either of us were single and found a fabulous fuck, we did the same. One of us had him until we were bored, then let the other take over. Mostly it was just one night each, sometimes – like Danny – it lasted a couple of weeks. We were never caught out – and I got plenty of my new-found love, anal sex. Annie certainly knew how to pick guys who were very, very good at it. But I never thought we'd fuck the same man on the same night – until Stefano turned up.

It was a summer afternoon – one of those days when it's so hot that all you want to do is lie about in a bikini drinking chilled cocktails. Unfortunately my job for the day was to sit in and wait for our new fridge to be delivered. About as unsexy an afternoon as you could get. We'd tossed a coin to see which one of us should stay home, and I'd lost. 'Between 9am and 6pm, love,' was as accurate as the chirpy cockney delivery guy on the phone could get.

'Can't you give me any idea?' I wailed. Annie and a couple of our friends were hitting the local pizza bar for a long, leisurely, wine-fuelled Saturday lunch, and I was desperate to join them.

'Sorry, love,' he chirped. 'Stacks of deliveries, all over the South East. And you know the M25. Now just last week at Junction 7…'

'Okay, thanks,' I said hastily. 'See you when you get here.' I hung up.

'I told you we should have paid for a proper delivery firm,' I grumbled.

'No chance,' said Annie. 'My friend at work uses this one. They're a quarter of the price. And they're the only ones who would come on a Saturday. You don't want to waste a day's holiday on it, do you?'

She was right. I didn't. And just as I suspected, there was no sign of the delivery guy by the time Annie set off for the restaurant. 'Phone me when he shows up,' Annie called as she disappeared out of the front door. 'Maybe you'll get there in time for coffee.'

'Maybe,' I replied, through gritted teeth. My experience of waiting for deliveries usually meant a wasted day, ending in total frustration when they didn't even turn up.

By 6pm there was still no sign of my fabulous fridge and I was so wound up and irritated that I considered making a long and furious telephone call to complain when Annie called to say she'd left the restaurant and gone along to the pub.

'Just come down,' she insisted. 'He's obviously not going to show up now.'

'Okay,' I sighed. 'I'll get changed. I'm still in my bikini.'

At that moment, the doorbell rang.

'He's here,' I snapped down the phone, pulling my sarong around my lower half. 'About bloody time too. I could have had lunch with you guys and come back by now.'

I put down the phone and wrenched open the front door, quietly seething. 'What time do you call…' I began, and stopped dead in my tracks. Think Matthew Fox with ever bigger biceps and you've got him. One hell of a hunk, standing right there on my doorstep, in pale denim jeans and a white T-shirt, pulled tight over his wide, firm pecs. His eyes were dark brown, deep set with heavy, come-to-bed lids, his hair short and dark, and his tanned skin had a ruddy, warm glow to it. He smelled of cigarettes and espresso – not an aroma that would usually drive me wild, but somehow it suited him. The attraction between us was instant and intense. For a split second his eyes automatically flicked sexily over me, lingering on my tits, perfectly cupped by my pink bikini top. That sexy look turned my anger into a beaming smile, before he flicked back, businesslike, to his clipboard.

'American fridge-freezer?' he asked, scanning down his list, revealing a trace of an accent I couldn't place.

'Yes,' I gushed, opening the door right up. 'I'm Debbie.'

'Stefano,' he replied, with a smile. This was the hottest guy I'd met for months, and just looking at him was making me wet. Suddenly it was worth staying in all day just for a glimpse of him. Lust was written all over my face, no matter how much I tried to hide it. My nipples were hard, clearly visible through the fabric of my bikini top. And I could see the arousal reflected in his eyes and smile too, though there was no visible bulge in his jeans, yet. We wanted each other very badly.

'You're Italian?' I blurted it out, just for something to say, desperate to keep him talking. All I could think about was unzipping those trousers and revealing what I knew would be an absolutely magnificent cock. There was something about Stefano's confidence, the way he looked at me, that told me he'd certainly know just how to use it.

'Si.' He grinned. '*Italiano.*'

'I'm afraid the only Italian I know is "cappuccino",' I giggled, wishing I could pull myself together and stop sounding like a silly schoolgirl. When it came to guys I was usually so in control, but Stefano's sexy smile and beautiful body had got me pretty hot and bothered.

He looked back at his van, and beckoned to a skinny student-type in dirty jeans, who wheeled a simply enormous box up the front path.

'Straight through for the kitchen,' I told him, stepping out on to the doorstep with Stefano to let him pass. My hand brushed against Stefano's, sending a rush of desire through every nerve in my body. I wanted his hand to touch every part of me, to stroke, to massage, to pleasure. Just the thought made my nipples and clit tingle, craving his touch, aching for him, and I knew then that I had to have him. Right there, right then.

The other guy wheeled his empty trolley past us and back to the van.

'You'll need to sign this,' Stefano said, handing me the clipboard. 'Do you have a pen?'

It was now or never. 'I've got one inside,' I replied. 'Do you want to come in while I find it?'

He knew exactly what I meant, because he ran back to the van to speak to the skinny guy, and as soon as we were through the front door, he closed it behind us. We walked into the kitchen and my mouth was on his in a moment, kissing, biting, drinking in his taste of coffee and cigarettes. His hands were on his belt, undoing it and forcing his jeans down on to the floor, revealing a delicious, uncircumcised cock, fully erect, thick and long, its veins so engorged with blood that they stood out like a road map. I copied him, untying my sarong and easing my bikini bottoms to the floor.

'Are you ready for me?' he asked, sliding his fingers between my soaking pussy lips.

'You know I am,' I gasped, as his rough forefinger rasped over and over my clit. He lifted me up under the arms and sat me on top of the washing machine, my wet pussy perched right on the very edge. With one hand on his cock, he slid it up and down between my lips, stimulating my clit with the swollen, shiny head, which felt so much smoother and sexier than his rough hands. I was close to coming, and he knew it, so he plunged his cock deep into my cunt over and over again, his balls slapping against my thighs and the base of his cock now stimulating my aching clit. He fucked me like that for a minute, then dropped to his knees and licked my bud, tracing the edges of my pussy lips with his tongue. Each time I was a second or two away from orgasm, he sensed it and stopped for a few seconds, just enough to let the moment pass. I had never, ever, been so turned on in my life. But

I wanted him to come in my arse. I turned on to my front, so I was bent over the washing machine, and shoved my arsehole in the air.

'This I have never done,' he whispered.

A virgin. An anal virgin. Just the thought almost made me come on the spot. He was going to ease that cock into his first ever arsehole, and he was going to love it. 'I'm wet,' I replied. 'And I'm ready. Fuck me in the arse, Stefano. Fuck me now.'

He did as he was told, and I bit my lip as he speared into me, ignoring the brief moment of pain. Stefano let out a stream of Italian words – it could have been anything, but it was deeply sexy. It was quick – maybe only four or five thrusts – and his hot cum spurted into my arsehole, filling me up.

'I'm sorry, baby,' he whispered. 'You have not come yet.' And with that he pulled his cock from my arse and plunged it, semi-erect, into my dripping cunt from behind, rubbing my clit with that rough forefinger. A trickle of cum seeped from my arsehole and down the back of my legs. Stefano knew I was way past the point of no return and I didn't want to hold back my orgasm this time, so he fingered my clit as fast as he could, until the hot waves of total satisfaction shuddered through my sore, sensitive body.

His limp dick slid from my pussy.

'I cannot believe how good that was,' he replied, turning me to face him and kissing me gently on the lips. 'Thank you.'

'There's a first time for everything.' I smiled. 'Take a quick shower if you want. The bathroom's through there.'

He disappeared into the bathroom and I heard the power shower burst into life. I pulled up my bikini bottoms, my cunt and arsehole sore but satisfied. Thank God I'd been the one who had to sit in all day. That fuck was so worth it. I wondered vaguely if he made a habit of screwing his customers. If so, no wonder he was so late. We'd never see each other again, that was for sure, and I wished Annie had been able to experience it.

I made a pot of coffee, and glanced out of the window, where the van was still parked, with the skinny guy asleep on the passenger seat.

Suddenly I heard the key in the front door and Annie walked in.

'It's huge!' she exclaimed, staring at the giant box in the kitchen. Then she saw my flushed face. 'Jeez, you didn't have to lift it on your own, did you?'

I laughed, as a wicked thought popped into my head. 'There's a delivery driver in the shower who's probably ready to go again, if you're up for it.' I grinned. 'He's an anal virgin – or rather, he was until about ten minutes ago. I think he's a big fan now. Trust me, he's gorgeous.

And Italian.'

Annie's eyes lit up. 'Do you think we'll get away with it?'

'Only one way to find out! By the way, he's called Stefano.'

'Might as well,' she said. 'It's been weeks.'

She disappeared into her bedroom and emerged seconds later in a bikini identical to mine. She rapped on the bathroom door, and Stefano's muffled voice called out: 'Yeah, I'm nearly done... Unless pretty baby wants some more, huh?'

I heard my sister step into the shower. 'More, Stefano, than you'll ever know.'

I picked up a magazine and my coffee, and retreated into my room, where I planned to stay until our delivery boy lover was gone. I smiled to myself at our little secret and the knowledge of what Annie was about to enjoy.

CURTAIN RAISER

We've all got those unwritten boundaries in our heads, the ones that tell us certain sexy antics are a step too far. But how can we judge something unless we've experienced it for ourselves? Cathy didn't think this kind of sex was for her — until she tried it. So sit back, read on and imagine yourself in her situation. It's pretty damn horny, isn't it? I thought so. I still get off on it.

It was a typical Sunday morning and Cathy stretched out on the bed, her body cosy and snug under the white cotton duvet in the bedroom of her smart, first-floor Victorian flat. Last night's cocktail dress was draped over the dressing-table chair, the winter sun weakly slanting through the half-open blinds and her boyfriend, David, fast asleep beside her. She rolled over and traced his face with her eyes, relishing the sight of his long, dark lashes and rugged, handsome features. David was most definitely the hottest guy she'd ever been out with. And the sex was, frankly, just mind-blowing. Like Cathy, he was up for pretty much anything.

They'd been together for almost a year, ever since meeting through an online dating agency. Too many people thought agencies were for sad, lonely people who didn't have a hope in hell of pulling a decent guy if they went to a bar, Cathy thought. She'd joined because her busy lifestyle – she was a highly successful film and TV make-up artist – meant she didn't have time to trawl bars hoping to pick up hot men. Sure, she met plenty of people through work, but Cathy found that the best ones were either taken, gay, or both. Besides, Cathy had one rule when it came to work – never ever mix business with pleasure. Cathy was very blonde, very petite and stunningly pretty, and some of the hottest celebrities on both sides of the Atlantic had made it clear they were up for more than just a quick dusting with the powder brush. Several of them were in very high-profile relationships. The sort you often see splashed across the cover of tabloid papers. Turning them down hadn't been easy, but not even the thought of the thousands of pounds she'd command selling her story had been enough – or the kick she'd get from sucking off the most desired men on the planet. Cathy loved her job, enjoyed her lifestyle, but she didn't want the whole showbiz world to be part of her home life too.

So she'd given the online dating agency a whirl, and

after a couple of spectacularly bad dates, she'd met David, who was a stunningly attractive, straight-talking, no-nonsense junior doctor. Like her, he was worried his dates would be weird, mad or bad, but they'd just clicked. The moment she saw him, she wanted him. By the end of the night they were fucking each other on her kitchen work-top, his gorgeous thick cock pressed hard into her cunt – and had been together ever since. David was Mr Right-for-now, and maybe even Mr Right if it went on long enough.

Desperate for a coffee, Cathy slid her legs on to the soft white carpet, pulled her fluffy white robe around her and padded to the kitchen. Cathy opened the ground coffee and tipped several huge spoonfuls into the cafetiere. Now that she was upright, her head was throbbing slightly, reminding her just how much they'd had to drink the night before. She reached into the cupboard and pulled out two coffee cups, a bowl of sugar and a couple of aspirins.

The memories of last night came to her in flashbacks as she ran the cold water tap and swigged back the painkillers with water. Meeting for a drink in that bar. Then that gorgeous little Thai restaurant in town. The one with the low-level red lighting and velvet seats. What was it she'd had to eat? She couldn't remember. Drinking too much wine. Wandering out into the city streets hoping to hail a cab home.

That was when he'd said it.

She poured boiling water into the cafetiere and stirred it vigorously before ramming on the top a little too hard, sending coffee and grounds spilling all over the granite kitchen worktop, as she struggled to remember his exact words, the precise look on his face. They'd taken a detour through Soho, a seedier part of the West End, and down a street lined with neon signs flashing: 'Sex shop', 'Peep show', 'Adult mags'. Girls in kiosks at the front of shops, their huge tits spilling out of their low-cut tops, inviting people to 'come in and see the show'. Thick-set security guys – or maybe pimps, probably both – hovered in the background, not wanting to come too close and dissuade the punters, but visible enough for people to know not to mess with the girls or try and sneak in without paying. David was very drunk, and so was Cathy. For some reason, she'd glanced over at him, just as they passed the entrance to an especially seedy sex show. He was looking at the entrance, just a small doorway with some tatty blue lino on the floor and one of those cheap beaded room dividers hanging over it. Cathy could tell that her boyfriend was horny. She could see it in his eyes. And when she glanced down, the beginnings of an erection bulged in his trousers.

'Want to go in?' she'd asked, feeling mildly jealous and surprised.

For a second, he'd looked embarrassed. Then he'd stopped, turned to face her and whispered: 'I want to fuck you in there.'

Cathy was pretty shocked. But it wasn't only David's suggestion that shocked her. It was the fact that when he said it, she'd felt a warm shiver of excitement rush through her. This was something she'd never even thought of doing before. The idea of even going into a peep show, with God knows what on the floor or who in the cubicle beside you, peering through a tiny crack in the wall at a woman pretending to masturbate – had never occurred to Cathy. It was the preserve of men in raincoats who didn't stand a hope of a decent fuck unless they paid for it, surely? But here she was, with a perfectly respectable, gorgeous man who was getting a kick out of the idea – and to her complete surprise, so was she.

Cathy glanced over at the doorway, mesmerised. Between her legs she felt a spreading patch of dampness, soaking through her panties and into her jeans. That doorway was the entrance to another world, one of pure lust, where nothing mattered except total physical satisfaction. Suddenly, in that moment, Cathy could see what was attractive about it. Through that doorway was a world of total anonymity. No words, no love, no relationships, just lust. She pressed her legs together, a trickle of her juices seeping down the inside of her thigh.

Had she replied to David's suggestion? She honestly couldn't remember. Had the look on her face told him she was horny too? She couldn't be sure. All she could remember was that they'd caught a cab home and had urgent, passionate sex before falling into a blissful sleep.

Cathy plonked the two mugs of coffee on a tray and wished she'd remembered to buy croissants. Never mind, she thought, a packet of chocolate digestives will have to do, and returned to the bedroom where David was just waking up.

'Baby,' he said, as she placed the coffee and biscuits on the bedside table. 'You were wild last night.'

'Was I?' she replied, catching a glimpse of her bed-head hair in the mirror. 'I'd had so much to drink that I really can't remember.'

For a split second a look of relief washed over David's face. 'I know,' he said, grinning, as she slid into bed beside him. 'We did knock back a few. I, er, can't remember much either.'

His hand was between her thighs in an instant, the side of his palm gently pressing against her bud. Cathy felt for his cock and slid down under the covers, her mouth hungry for him. 'I don't think you're anywhere near hard enough,' she whispered, running her tongue all the way up his shaft from the base to the tip, easing back his foreskin to reveal the beautiful, shiny pink head. Her mouth was on him in a second, taking his gorgeous cock into her throat, and they fucked, licked and sucked each other all morning, the thought of going to that peep show secretly on both their minds.

❧

Days passed, and David never mentioned the peep show. Nor did Cathy. But thoughts of what they could do in there consumed her. When they fucked, an imaginary sex show went on in her head. When David stayed at his place, Cathy masturbated furiously to thoughts of it, almost wearing out the batteries of her Rabbit vibrator. Eventually, she couldn't resist walking home one night, on the pretext that it would be better exercise than taking her usual tube ride, but in fact so that she could walk down that very street of brothels and titty bars like they had on Friday night.

The street was quite narrow, just big enough for two cars to pass, and the pavements were crammed with people making their way home from work, to bars and clubs, or just wandering past the sex shops for a look. Cathy wasn't exactly sure where the peep show was. Then she spotted it.

There wasn't much to see. Just a door in a wall, with 'Girls – Live!' in red neon lights above it, and a tatty red-

and-white beaded curtain. Outside, a girl leaned against the wall, the orange streetlamps illuminating her heavily made-up face. Probably in her late 20s, Cathy decided, though with so much make-up it was hard to tell. She was wearing a low-cut white shirt, micro skirt which gave a glimpse of her lacy panties, and the tallest black stilettos Cathy had ever seen. The girl took a long drag on a cigarette and chatted casually to one of the 'security' guys lurking in the shadows beside her. Cathy realised she was probably one of the 'performers' on a break. She was skinny, with long, poker-straight black hair down to her waist, and thick, dark red lipstick. Not beautiful, more sort of sexy in a hard, worn way. But the thought of seeing this girl naked through a peep hole, watching her slender fingers flicking her clit, while David's swollen cock thrust in and out of her, made Cathy shiver with excitement. She'd never touch the girl, and she didn't want to. This was about watching, letting her eyes feast on another girl's tits and cunt. Cathy tried not to stare, and strolled past as casually as she could, but as the girl looked up their eyes met. Embarrassed, Cathy looked away, pulled her mobile phone from her bag and fiddled with the keys, pretending to read a text, as if she was far too busy and important to be interested in a sex club. The girl smiled to herself knowingly, and took another drag on her cigarette.

The tube ride home seemed to take forever, but it

gave Cathy a chance to make up her mind. This was more than a fantasy. She had to make it happen, or every waking moment would be filled with fantasies of it. David was up for it when drunk, she knew that for sure, but how would he react if she suggested it to him when sober? After all, it wasn't every day your girlfriend says: 'Hi honey, I'm home! Whaddya sat to fucking me senseless inside a Soho sex joint?' And what if one of his patients saw him? More than that, what if any of her friends saw them? Cathy liked to keep her sexual habits to herself.

She stopped at the off licence and bought a bottle of wine. By the time David arrived she'd drunk half of it. He poured himself a large glass and flopped down on the sofa. Cathy curled up beside him. She couldn't stop herself. She'd planned to wait until he'd had at least a couple of glasses, but the wine had given her courage and there was no backing out now. If she wanted to make her fantasy happen, this was her big chance.

'You know the other night, when we went past that peep show...' she began, looking up at him.

David interrupted her, his face reddening. 'Sweetheart, I'm really sorry. I didn't mean it. I'd just had a lot to drink, that's all.'

'Have you ever done that before? Gone in one, I mean. A peep show. With someone?'

'God, no!' he replied, an embarrassed smile spreading over his face. 'I've never even been brave enough to go in on my own.'

Cathy snuggled closer. 'So you do want to,' she said. 'Maybe we should try it sometime,' she whispered, between kisses. 'Go there together. I went past it tonight and just the thought of it made me wet.'

Her hand was resting on his crotch, and as she spoke she felt his cock stiffen instantly. 'I'll take that as a yes, then,' she said, smiling.

'How about now?' David whispered, so horny that his hand was already inside his trousers, wanking his cock roughly. 'Let's go down there right now.' His hand moved faster and faster until it was a blur, unable to let go of his throbbing, swollen cock. Cathy knew instinctively what was going on. This was David's ultimate fantasy, and by suggesting it she'd made him uncontrollably horny. She watched him masturbate, leaning back on the sofa and yanking his cock out of his trousers, harder and rougher than she'd ever seen before, feeling utterly thrilled that just a few words from her had driven him into a sexual frenzy. Even though she was horny as hell, she didn't want to come here. This was one orgasm she wanted to delay, until she was living her fantasy.

'I can't stop, I've got to come,' David gasped. Cathy sensed he was passing the point of no return. She lowered her lips over the purple head, and with one suck from Cathy he filled her mouth with his delicious, salty cum, shooting out so hard that it hit the back of her throat. Cathy swallowed every drop, apart from a trickle that leaked from the edge of her mouth, which she swept up with her finger. Her own clitoris was throbbing, she was so close to her climax, but she wanted to wait. She had to. Holding back her own orgasm would just make it even better when she finally came. It took all her energy to stop herself massaging that cum-covered finger on her clit – just one touch of his juices on hers would have sent waves of pleasure crashing through her – but somehow Cathy did it. She slipped her finger into his mouth and he sucked on the taste of himself, licking every drop.

'I don't know what came over me!' He grinned, his wet fingers reaching for Cathy's clit.

'No!' she said, pushing his hand away a little more forcefully than she meant to. 'Sorry, I didn't mean… It's just I want to come in that peep show. It'll be even better if I wait.'

'Let's go!' he said, zipping up his trousers. 'Trust me, it won't matter that I've already come. I'm getting hard again just thinking about it.'

They hailed a cab outside the flat and half an hour later stepped out in the centre of town, a short stroll from the peep show. Neither spoke on the way – too excited, too horny, too nervous to talk. Cathy was about to step into the unknown, a brand new world where she didn't know what to expect. Where did you pay? How much was it? How long did you get? What if someone they knew saw them? But if she was honest with herself, the chance of entering the unknown, of being seen, of getting 'caught', added to the thrill.

They took the cab to a still fairly commercial area with bars, shops and restaurants, but within walking distance of the red-light district. Light, thin rain was beginning to fall, sparkling in the streetlights, and the neon signs coming into view seemed brighter and more exciting than ever to Cathy.

'Which one shall we go in?' David asked. 'What about this one?'

He walked towards a shop front which, beyond an extensive range of porn mags and shelves of sex toys, had a small entrance with cheesy music and lurid, dark red light emanating from it. 'No,' Cathy replied, pulling him back. 'I know exactly which one. Where you first suggested it. It's down here. That's the one in my fantasy.'

They made their way down the side-street to the entrance. The girl had gone, and in her place, standing by the wall, was a thick-set guy in a badly fitting suit.

'Walk straight in,' Cathy whispered, her heart pounding with the thrill of it all. 'Don't hesitate. Straight in.

We've got to get in quickly. You never know, someone we know might walk past.'

'Okay,' he replied, heading straight for the beaded curtain. 'I'll go in first.'

He barged straight through, displaying an outer confidence that Cathy knew he didn't really have. Like her, this was a new situation, one where you were breaking your own rules. Cathy followed him down a dimly lit corridor with a desk at the end. Behind it sat a middle-aged woman, her deeply lined face thick with make-up. She gave them a tired smile. For a moment Cathy had the awful feeling that this woman was one of the performers. The mildly horrified look on David's face told her he was thinking the same.

'Do you need pound coins?' she asked.

David nodded, handing her a £20 note. She gave him a bag of coins, and jerked a thumb towards a corridor behind her.

'Down there,' she added. 'Any cubicle with the curtain open.'

The first three cubicles were occupied, or at least the grubby-looking curtains were closed, but the fourth was empty. Half horny, half anxious, Cathy followed David inside and pulled the curtain shut behind her. It was seedy, dark and hot, with peeling wallpaper and a damp, earthy smell, just as Cathy had fantasised; pure lust stripped bare. She could hear tinny music, and in front of them there was a coin machine and a slot the size of a letterbox. Her heart thumped harder and louder than she'd ever felt it before and beads of sweat dripped down between her tits.

'Put the money in,' she urged. With trembling fingers, he slid five pound coins into the slot.

The letterbox flap slid sideways and Cathy peered through. It was the girl. The one with the poker-straight black hair. She was dancing on a small platform under a spotlight, with a large mirror behind her. She was topless, her beautiful, small, firm tits thrust forwards towards their booth. As Cathy watched, the dancer unzipped her micro skirt and let it fall to the floor, exposing her white lace knickers, her tight arse reflected in the mirror. The girl licked and sucked her fingers and ran them over her hard nipples. Just the sight of the girl's fingers sliding in and out of her red-lipsticked mouth made Cathy wet. Her own clit began to swell, sending shockwaves of desire through every inch of her body. Instinctively, she slipped her hand up her skirt and rubbed it through her under-wear.

'What can you see?' asked David. Cathy was so over-whelmed by the moment that she'd forgotten he was there.

She moved aside slightly so that David could look

through the letterbox too. His hand went to his cock, and he and Cathy stood side-by-side. The girl lowered her panties and bent over right in front of their peep-hole, her wet pink cunt and sexy arsehole just a metre away. Cathy let out a gasp as she grew closer to her orgasm. She imagined what it would be like to lick that cunt, to plunge her fingers deep into it, to probe inside that beautiful arse. The stickiness of the floor under her feet, knowing that so many men had shot their spunk onto that dirty, cracked lino while watching the show, made Cathy's clit throb almost painfully.

Suddenly, the letterbox snapped shut.

'Money, David!' gasped Cathy, desperately. 'Put in more money. The coins! Quick!'

He tore his hand from his swollen cock and fed a handful of pound coins into the machine as fast as he could. The letterbox snapped open, and for a second Cathy found herself looking directly into the dancer's eyes. The girl gave her a half-smile and looked away. The girl recognised immediately that she'd looked into the eyes of a young woman, the type of punter she didn't get too often, and something told Cathy she was going to give her a really good show. The girl sat down on the stage with her legs stretched wide open, heels digging into the wooden floor, and began rubbing her clit fast and hard. A dribble of juice trickled from her cunt – whether it was her juice or someone's cum, Cathy wasn't sure – but she knew the dancer was genuinely horny. She was masturbating for real.

David saw it too. He didn't need to watch any more. She felt David's hands around her hips, yanking down her thong, and she realised how badly she needed him inside her. He plunged into her from behind, no longer watching the dancer, thrusting his thick cock in as deep as he could, leaving Cathy to watch the girl, who was squeezing her pussy lips together as her finger made rapid circular movements on her clit. Suddenly the girl's body trembled as she came, and Cathy's body, too, rocked with orgasm, her cunt gripping on to David's cock, her eyes wide open and fixed on the girl's delicious bud. His own climax, deep inside Cathy, came seconds later, his fingernails scratching her hips.

Cathy closed her eyes for a moment, relishing every second of what had been the most extraordinary sexual experience of her life. The peep-hole slammed shut and David pulled out of her, sending cum and her own juices pouring down her thighs. There was a box of tissues attached to the wall, so Cathy took a handful and cleaned herself up. They looked at each other and smiled.

'That was incredible,' he said, kissing her forehead. 'You've just made my fantasy come true.'

'Put another pound in,' Cathy urged. 'I want to see

what she's doing now.'

David fed another pound into the meter and when the letterbox snapped open, the girl was dancing again, her panties and micro-skirt back on, her fingers circling her nipples. She looked straight at the letterbox and smiled. Then Cathy heard a thud as the slot in the cubicle beside them slid open. The girl ran a wet finger over her panties as she danced, but there was a bored, distracted look in her eyes and Cathy knew that this punter had missed the real show.

The viewing slot in their cubicle snapped shut for the last time. Cathy and David straightened their clothes, slipped quickly out of the doorway and back into the everyday world, where they were a nice middle-class couple. No-one would dream they'd fuck in a peep show. And Cathy smiled to herself, knowing this was the first of many sexual adventures where they'd push the unwritten boundaries to their limits.

FATHER FIGURE

It takes a strong woman to follow where her lust leads – and an even stronger one to keep going past society's taboos. Jane did just that, and was rewarded with an orgasmic experience she'll never forget. And neither will I – the scenes she described to me the night we shared a drink in a hotel bar are often in my fantasies, and I'm sure they'll soon be in yours, too...

'Time, ladies, please,' implored the barman for the third time as Jane tipped the last of the Pinot Grigio into her glass.

'Well, if you ask me,' went on her best friend Trish, 'I think he's a bastard. All this talk about "giving him another chance" is utter bullshit.'

'I agree,' chipped in Fiona. 'A top-rank, number one, complete and utter arsehole. You're better off without him, Jane. And you'd even talked about getting engaged. Met the family and everything. What a sod. Don't even think about going there again.'

Jane took a huge swig of wine. 'Ladies, I agree.' She

raised her glass. 'To being single!'

The girls were right, and Jane knew it. Simon was an arsehole. They'd been together for over a year – until a week ago, when Trish had spotted him holding hands and canoodling with his ex-girlfriend in a restaurant. Trish – not one to hold back – had walked over and deposited a glass of red wine on his head, much to the amusement of fellow diners.

'That's for being a two-timing bastard,' she'd announced, as Simon stared at her speechlessly and his ex made a hasty exit to the loos. Then she'd called Jane, told her not to answer her phone to Simon, and gone straight round to tell her in person.

He'd turned up, of course, with a huge bouquet of flowers and the classic sob story. 'She's just split up with her boyfriend,' he insisted, looking up at Jane from the doorstep with his huge brown eyes and his longish brown hair flopping over them. 'Needed a shoulder to cry on. I – I got carried away. I was stupid. There's nothing going on, Jane, honest. I love you. My whole family loves you.'

It would be so easy to forgive him, Jane had thought to herself. When Simon turned on the charm, resisting was almost impossible. Not to mention the amazing sex. Simon had the biggest, thickest cock she'd ever seen, and, like her, he'd happily give oral for hours. Jane loved nothing more than sucking on his huge, fat dick, knowing that when she was ready he'd pound it inside her, satisfying her cunt and clitoris at the same time with its enormous girth. But she'd stayed strong. 'Forget it,' she'd snapped, closing the door in his face. 'We're finished.'

So here she was – free and single again, and already missing Simon. Mostly, though, as she began to realise, she was missing the sex. When she came to think about it, sex was really all they'd had in common. Both of them had a high libido, loving to fuck as often as possible, in as many places as they could think of. In the past, Jane had found that her boyfriends couldn't keep up with her urges. Simon was as up for it as she was.

'He was just so good in bed,' she said, as the girls gave the barman a cheery wave, put on their coats and headed out to the taxi rank. 'I've told you about his…'

'Yeah, yeah, yeah, we've heard!' chorused the girls, hoping to drown out yet another graphic description of Simon's enormous member. 'I know, love,' comforted Trish, 'but there are tons of guys out there who are good in bed, and they don't all go around lusting after their ex-girlfriends. You've just got to forget him and give someone else a chance. He can't be the only person in the world with a massive knob!' The girls shrieked and Jane smirked to herself. Trish was right. They joined the taxi queue and were chatting about arranging a girlie holiday to the Maldives when Jane felt a tap on her shoulder.

'Hello, Jane,' said a deep, well-spoken voice. She turned and her eyes fell on a familiar face.

'Chris! My goodness, how are you?' she replied. 'What are you doing here?'

'I've been out with some old workmates.'

Jane kissed him on both cheeks. 'Everyone, this is Chris,' she announced. 'Simon's dad.'

A few of the girls groaned at the mention of Simon and burbled tipsy comments about 'the love-rat swine'. Chris shrugged and pulled an apologetic, hangdog expression, putting them all at ease. The girls shook hands with him, as Jane desperately tried to work out how long he'd been there and whether she'd been in full-on rant about Simon. No, she decided, by the time they were in that queue the conversation had most definitely been on holidays. Jane noticed just how gorgeous Chris was the very first time that she met him. She'd never been one for older men, and Chris was in his late 40s – 20 years older than her – but he was a more rugged, well-built version of Simon, with a deeper, sexier voice. He had the same cute, baby-blue eyes, the same floppy dark hair – though his was flecked with grey. She'd been to dinner a couple of times with him and Simon, and afterwards, on both nights, when she'd fucked Simon, she'd fantasised that she was being screwed by his father. It was one of those off-limits fantasies that she'd always felt a little bit guilty about afterwards.

'Sorry to hear about you and Si,' he went on. 'The lad brings it on himself.'

'Thanks,' Jane replied. 'So, how's your new girlfriend? Sam, was it? The one we met when Si and I came over.'

'Fine, I think. But she's not my girlfriend any more. Things didn't work out. I'm back on the market again, if there is a market for old has-beens.'

Jane giggled. At least he was self-deprecating. Simon took himself so seriously all the time, while his dad was far more laid-back and easy-going, able to laugh at himself. That was one of the things she admired about him. The queue shuffled forwards and as they chatted, and began to flirt just a little, Jane found herself fancying him more and more. For a split second, Jane wondered if he had the same... No, she wouldn't even go there in her mind. This was Simon's dad, for God's sake! Way off-limits.

They reached the front of the queue and Trish and Fiona climbed into their cab. Jane was going the other way. Her mind was in turmoil. With her and Simon over for good, she'd never see Chris again. It was just chance that they'd bumped into each other. But how on earth could she take things further? And did she really want to?

The damp patch spreading in her panties told her the answer. Just chatting to him had brought her to a state of arousal, her clit tingling pleasantly. She could either say goodbye, go home and masturbate – or she could dive into the unknown. That would be one way to put Simon behind her for good.

'We could share a cab, if you like,' she blurted out. 'My flat's in Notting Hill. It's not that far from you.'

It wasn't true, and Chris knew it. Going via her flat would mean a detour of about half an hour.

'Sure,' he replied, those blue eyes sparkling. 'That'd be great.'

He held the door open for her and she slid into the back seat, the leather cold on her bare legs. Such a gentleman, just like Simon. Chris climbed in beside her. He was wearing an aftershave she couldn't place, but she liked it.

'Highgate,' she told the driver, leaning forward to speak to him through the glass partition. 'Via Notting Hill.'

He gave her a puzzled look, clearly wondering why anyone in Central London would share a cab when one was going North and the other West. But her eyes flashed dangerously, and realising the score, he replied: 'Of course, love,' and snapped the sliding window shut.

Jane kept the conversation light, but the sexual tension between them was hitting boiling point. She wanted Chris so badly, more than she'd ever wanted Simon, because there was something so deliciously naughty about the thought of fucking him, and because she didn't know if she'd have the guts to go through with it.

Driven by your typical London cabbie, the taxi bounced along the streets, the driver taking sharp turns. Jane used each bounce and jerk to secretly edge closer and closer to Chris and rested her head sideways on his shoulder, feigning tiredness.

'Are you sleepy, baby?' he whispered.

She looked up at his face so their lips brushed together. The ache in her clit had spread throughout her whole body, so that every inch of her craved his touch. For a few seconds they stayed frozen, both of them knowing that this was their only chance to back out, to say goodbye and not take that step. But neither of them could say no. It was just a question of who was going to make the first move.

'You know I want you,' Chris whispered. 'I'm just not sure if...'

She answered him with a kiss, her tongue probing inside his mouth, exploring every inch, sliding in and out, loving the warm wetness she found there. Unlike Simon, who would have instantly made a grab for her tits, Chris focused on kissing her back, slowly and gently, expertly exploring her mouth with his own tongue, just the way she hoped he'd explore her pussy when they got home. He was clearly a very experienced lover, and the thought of how good he'd be in bed made her shiver. But kissing each other was one thing, full-blown sex quite another.

'We shouldn't be doing this...' Chris panted, his hand moving involuntarily down to her tits, kneading them through her dress before pulling it away again.

'It's okay, Chris,' she whispered, taking his hand and resting it back on her tit. 'I want you to do this. I'm so turned on that my pussy is soaked.'

Chris let out a gasp, his hand dropped to his lap and his body trembled. Then he said: 'I'm so sorry.' At first she thought he couldn't go through with it. But when she looked down, his trousers were damp. She'd turned him on so much that he'd come prematurely. Jane smiled inwardly. Coming too soon was one of Simon's little habits – in the end they'd agreed that he'd always have a wank ten minutes before, so he could keep going for longer. It looked like nature had repeated itself.

'It's fine, Chris, really,' she replied, lowering her face into his lap and inhaling his musk, feeling his semi-erect cock resting on her face through the now-glossy fabric. To her delight, his cock felt easily as huge as Simon's. Bigger, if that were possible. 'It's still twenty minutes to my flat. You'd better be ready to go again by the time we arrive, that's all.'

He smiled gratefully, and buried his face in her cleavage, licking her nipples through her silky dress. Jane pressed her legs together, squeezing her clit as much as she could to give herself some relief. By the time they reached her flat, Jane was more horny than she'd been before in her life. She was about to fuck someone she really shouldn't and that was quite possibly the hottest thing ever. They announced to the driver that this was the only stop and paid him quickly. They went straight into the bedroom, where only the previous week, Jane had sucked Simon off for the last time. The thought crossed her mind that she hadn't even changed the sheets – they'd still be stained with his cum – and it made her even hornier. Simon had moved out and luckily Jane had got rid of all her photos of him.

Now Chris took the lead, undressing her slowly, caressing every inch as he did so, so much more caring and tender than Simon. His body was wider, thicker, but in very good shape, and Jane realised that he worked out a lot – unlike Simon, who was rapidly developing a pot belly. Chris kissed all the way down from her nipples to her pussy, licking and nibbling as he went. His touch seemed so experienced, so expert; when he reached her bush he gently parted her pussy lips with his fingers and kissed all the way around her cunt.

'Lick my clit, please,' she begged. 'I'm so close. So close.'

He circled her clit with his tongue, but didn't touch it. 'Wait, baby,' he said, sliding one finger, then two, then four, into her cunt. 'Trust me, it'll be better this way. Wait for my cock to fuck you. When you finally come, it'll blow your mind.'

'I can't wait,' Jane begged, her whole body screamingly close to orgasm as he fisted her harder and harder, something Simon had never done.

'You can,' he replied, giving her clit one quick lick. Jane let out a wail of desire. She was just one more lick, one rub, one squeeze away from the orgasm that was about to engulf her.

'Lie back and spread your legs,' he whispered. 'Don't touch yourself. Don't move.'

Jane had never been this close to climax and managed to stop before. But she spread her legs and fought the urge to bring herself off with just a quick squeeze of her pussy. As she did so, Chris undid his shirt and trousers. Jane let out a gasp.

'Your cock is beautiful,' she told him, marvelling at it. 'It's the biggest I've ever seen.'

Chris's cock was a good inch longer than Simon's, and just as thick – so wide that her grip couldn't completely encircle it. She wasn't even sure if it would fit inside her – but she was sure as hell determined to find out.

'Fuck me, Chris,' she begged, squirming on the bed,

her legs as wide as she could stretch them, ready to take as much of that beautiful cock as she could, her pussy rapidly reaching the point of no return.

He eased his cock inside her, gently, inch by inch. 'Tell me when to stop,' he said. 'I don't want it to hurt.' So caring, so unlike his son.

On each thrust he pressed further into her cunt, until at last his entire dick was inside her, filling her completely. He rocked back and forth gently, his pubic bone pressing against her clit, but not pressing hard enough.

'Harder,' Jane begged. 'Fuck me properly, Chris. Fuck me hard.'

His rhythm sped up, and he pushed deeper and deeper, his pubes rough against her clit, each thrust sending a shooting, yet satisfying pain right through her. She gripped his arse with her hands, forcing him as deep as he could go, bearing the pain because she'd never felt so truly, deeply fucked. And she still couldn't believe it was Simon's dad who was doing it.

She'd had that cock in her cunt, and now she wanted him in her mouth. 'I've got to suck you off,' she gasped, pulling him down on to the bed and lowering her mouth over his throbbing member, sucking greedily. The purple head went so far back in her throat that it almost made her gag. Chris held her head as she rocked back and forth, both of them groaning with pleasure, as she took in as much of his cock as she could. He swivelled round so he could lick her pussy as she sucked him, and though his tongue felt so small after she'd had his cock in her, the feeling was still intense. Her orgasm came first. She finally surrendered to wave after wave of overwhelming, shuddering lust as he fucked her with his tongue, his fingers furiously massaging her clit. His own climax followed moments later and his delicious salty cum flowed into her mouth.

Jane and Chris collapsed in each other's arms on the bed, kissing each other as they shared their juices, hardly able to believe what they'd just done and knowing they'd never do it again. 'That was amazing,' Chris whispered. 'If it wasn't for Simon, I'd ask you out on a date.'

'And if it wasn't for Simon, I'd say yes,' she said.

Chris pulled her into his arms and kissed her tenderly. 'I know we shouldn't have done it, Jane, but I want you to know that I've never enjoyed sex as much as that.'

'Me neither,' replied Jane, as a momentary flash of delight passed over Chris's face, which he instantly suppressed, but Jane knew he'd got a kick out of knowing he was a far better fuck than his son.

COMING UP
ROSES

This girl's confession is really two stories in one – once her inner sex goddess was unleashed by another woman, she was eager to act out her deepest fantasy. I gasped when she told me what she did with those two gorgeous gardeners, and how she made her dream come true – I admit her words left me aroused for days...

It was always going to be a 'duvet day'. From the moment I opened my eyes that morning, I knew there was no way I could face the commute into work. And on top of that, it was my boss's leaving do. Don't get me wrong – I liked my job as a promotions manager. Loads of free trips abroad, plenty of freebie products and a great team of people. It was just that ever since that Christmas party I'd felt uncomfortable being around my boss.

She was gorgeous, no doubt about it. You didn't have to be gay to notice it. One of those people simply brimming with confidence, but not arrogant, and it was very sexy. She had shoulder-length dark hair, cut into a cute bob, a pretty turned-up nose and a body that was living proof she went to the gym several times a week. At work we all dressed down, and I loved the looks she chose, from combat trousers to girlie summer dresses. But I'd never thought of Cassie in that way. Not until the company's annual Christmas party.

I blame the drink. But if I'm honest, I think all the drink really did was unleash a latent sexual desire in me. I'd been brought up to be a 'good girl' – Catholic school, no sex before marriage (though by 18 I'd given up on that idea entirely) – and any lesbian lust I'd ever felt had been quickly, and subconsciously, pushed firmly to the back of my mind. Along with my ultimate fantasy of being fucked by two men at once. There were rumours that Cassie was bisexual, but I'd never really paid much attention to them. Cassie kept her private life to herself and I thought she was right to do so – her sex life was really no-one else's business.

I'd got to the party quite late, because unlike the other girls I lived quite near, so I'd gone home to get changed. They'd crammed in to the office loos with their party dresses, make-up and clouds of perfume. By the time I'd chatted to friends on the phone, lined my stomach with a fry-up and slipped into my favourite pink silk cocktail dress, the party had been in full swing for a good couple of hours.

The firm had hired a local club, and after negotiating security I made my way to the packed bar. Free drinks all night meant most people were determined to run up the biggest bar bill possible, and I joined them. After knocking back four cocktails in far-too-rapid succession, and chatting to some of my colleagues, I moved towards the dancefloor – and bumped into Cassie. She looked fantastic, in a black strapless cocktail dress, a single diamond pendant resting between her breasts. I'd never even noticed her tits before but, like the rest of her, they were beautifully in proportion, and the delicate necklace showed them off to perfection.

Normally at company socials I try and avoid management – I'm not the sort who tries to worm their way up the career ladder by becoming best mates over a drink or ten. But Cassie laid her prettily manicured fingers on my arm.

'Kara,' she said. 'I thought you weren't coming.'

'I went home first,' I explained. 'To change. I couldn't face trying to squeeze into the office loos.'

'I know what you mean,' she replied, her hand still resting delicately on my arm. 'You look beautiful, Kara.'

There was something about the way she said it that set an alarm bell ringing in my head. I covered my embarrassed pause with lots of chatter about work, but in my mind I couldn't stop hearing those words, that intonation in her voice, the way she'd laid that soft hand on the curve of my elbow. There was a look in her eyes, too – like me, she'd had a bit to drink, but it was an unmistakable look I'd only ever seen in guys before, one that meant they wanted to fuck you senseless.

The thought initially sent me into a panic. I wasn't the sort of girl who experimented that way. But what really panicked me were the overwhelming urges I felt every time I looked at her. If was as if, by touching my arm and smiling at me like that, Cassie had taken the lid off a whole area of my sexuality that I'd never even thought about, let alone explored. And now all I could think about as we talked was what it would be like to touch her, there, and to feel her beautiful fingers gently massaging my swelling bud.

My eyes just couldn't get enough of Cassie. We had a couple more drinks and began to flirt fairly openly though, as the club was so full, I didn't expect anyone to notice. As we chatted, we'd touch each other on the shoulder, or the arm, just a gentle, momentary brush, but it was igniting a hidden lust in me that I didn't know I had. Deep inside my pussy, I felt an ache, a longing for a woman's touch that I'd never known before. It was an incredible sexual awakening. Her perfume – Nina Ricci, I think – would forever remind me of that moment. My knickers were soaked, my nipples hard and ready for her delicate fingers and mouth to embrace them. I stopped trying to hide my feelings for her, or cover them with chatter, and silently met her gaze, as the sexual chemistry between us reached fever-pitch.

She leaned towards me and whispered: 'Would you like to go somewhere quieter?'

Clever girl, I thought. That's an innocent-enough sounding question, so if she'd mis-read my signals, or I changed my mind, it was easy for me to say no. But I didn't. I nodded, too horny to speak, and she turned and walked into one of the far, dark corners of the club. I was so nervous – I knew exactly what to do with a hard-on, but getting off with a woman was something I'd honestly never even thought about.

It was almost pitch black in the corner, but it was possible people could walk past, so I knew this would have to be quick. We were both taking such a risk, but the desire between us overcame all logic and reason. Cassie turned to face me and our lips were just an inch apart, her musk filling me with more desire than I'd ever thought possible.

'I'd like to touch you,' she said gently. 'Would you like me to?'

'Yes,' I breathed.

She kissed me gently, her mouth so soft and sensual

compared to a man's, and ran her fingers over my bush, through the dress. I let out a low moan as my pubes pressed on my bud, and Cassie knew I was ready for her fingers between my legs right there and then. Her hand slipped easily under my dress and up my right thigh. When she realised that I was wearing stockings it was her turn to moan. Cassie traced around the top of my stocking with her finger, just inside the elastic, my juices now dribbling down on to her hand.

'You are beautiful,' she whispered. 'I've wanted you ever since I first saw you.'

'It's my first time with a woman,' I whispered back.

Cassie moaned again, clearly overcome by the fact that this was a new experience for me. She took my hand and guided it between her legs, where her juices were warm and glossy on her inner thighs. She, too, was wearing stockings, and the feel of them drove me wild with desire. My fingers probed into her pussy through her soaked panties, entering virgin territory for me, loving the feel of her soft, wet sex, so much more delicate than a man's. Even her pubic hair felt gentler and softer. Cassie's fingers made gentle circles over my bud, touching me perfectly, with just enough pressure, and I copied her, using my middle finger to circle and massage her swollen clit. I explored her cunt, too, delving inside with my finger as her juices ran down it and over my hand. Our breasts were pressed against each other through the fabric of our dresses, my nipples on fire and longing for her to suck them. Her body tensed, and I knew she was close to coming, which brought me even closer. As she felt my pussy tense up around her finger, she withdrew it and whispered: 'Let's go outside.'

Cassie's hand took mine and a second later I was hit by a blast of the night air as she pushed open a fire door and led me into an empty courtyard at the back of the club. The rush of cool air of my bare skin made me feel even more alive, and we giggled as Cassie led me into a thin, deserted alleyway.

'And now,' she announced, 'I'm going to show you how much better a woman can be.'

She pushed my dress up to my waist and gripped my hips hard, her fingernails pressing and marking my flesh, as my back scraped against the rough wall. I bit my lip as the pain in my back seared for a moment, then my legs parted and her tongue delved into my cunt, licking and drinking my hot juices, and she sucked on my clit, making intense circles over and around it with her tongue. I lost control, unable to hold back the tension ready to be released from every muscle in my body, and my whole being rocked and bucked with the most delicious, intense orgasm I'd ever had. Cassie withdrew her mouth and kissed me all the way up the front of my dress, cupping my breast in her hand and slipping the nipple out of my dress so she could kiss it. Her hand was between her legs, stimulating her clit, and I knew she was happy to bring herself off, but I wanted to be the one to do it.

'It's your turn now,' I told her, turning her back to the wall so that she too could feel the scratches on her back. I didn't feel nervous any more, I felt exhilarated as I squatted in front of her, and eased her panties aside so I could slide my tongue into her crack. She began to pant with pleasure, rubbing her clit rapidly back and forth over my tongue, squeezing together her thighs to put maximum pressure on her pussy lips. Filled with new-found confidence, I eased a finger inside her, then two, then three, until all four were fucking her hard.

'I'm going to come, Kara,' she breathed. 'I'm going to come right here in your mouth.'

Her rhythm sped up even faster and I sucked her clit as hard as I could, until her body tensed and rocked with orgasm, just like mine had, her juices spurting into my mouth and I tasted the creamy cum. She jerked and jolted over and over, her cunt squeezing tight on my slippery fingers, until, finally, she lay back against the wall and laughed.

'If that was your first time,' she giggled, 'all I can say, Kara, is that you're a natural!'

We used some tissues out of Cassie's bag to clean ourselves up, and we didn't go back to the party, we shared a cab home. On the way back, I began to sober up and we didn't say much in the cab. I felt tense. I didn't regret what I'd done at all, but I wasn't sure if Cassie expected more – a repeat performance, a relationship perhaps – and I didn't want to go there. It was a perfect memory, an amazing experience, and I wanted to keep it that way. She was my boss, for God's sake. Her flat was the first stop, and thankfully Cassie didn't invite me in – it had clearly been a one-off for her, too.

'See you at work,' she said cheerfully, as she paid the driver her share.

I'd wanked over it as soon as I got home, licking what was left of her juices from my fingers and breathing in her smell. But I can't deny it was tricky at work. I found it difficult to work with her after that. Every time we were in a meeting together, I imagined my hand in her cunt, her body bucking in my mouth, and I couldn't concentrate on the job.

After a few days, Cassie took me aside. 'I'm moving to the States next week,' she confided. 'For good. New York office. It's been arranged for a while now. That's why I couldn't hold back at the party. It was my last chance to let go of all that pent-up lust!'

'I'm glad you did,' I replied with a grin.

I've got to admit I was pretty relieved. No matter what anyone says, it's not easy to work with someone you've fucked. And tonight was her leaving do. In the same club. That's why I was having a duvet day.

I called the office and said I wouldn't be in. Then I went back to bed with a pot of coffee and *Heat* magazine. As I flicked through the glossy pages, my eyes lingered on some of the very fit men – David Beckham especially – and admired some of the girls, too. Ever since my night with Cassie, I'd felt so much more open sexually. I hadn't had a man for a few months, but I knew that the next time I did, I'd be up for a lot more experimentation than before. And as for girls – well, if there was the right sexual vibe, who knows, I might be up for that too.

The sound of a chainsaw rasped through my ground-floor bedroom window and I got up, irritated, to see who the hell would create that kind of racket at 10am on a Friday morning. Outside, in the apartment block's communal gardens, were two men in their mid-20s. They were sawing up a tree-trunk which I guessed they'd cut down the previous week and clearing some old rose bushes. It was cool outside – no more than 12 or 13 degrees centigrade – but it was clearly hard work, because both guys had taken off their waterproof jackets and were working in T-shirts. I watched for a few moments, turned on by their huge, thick, muscular arms, shiny with sweat.

Neither of them were especially beautiful – I usually went for 'pretty boys' – but there was something so masculine, so strong about the way they hoisted the debris over their wide shoulders and walked across the wet grass with them that I couldn't stop watching. Both were very tall – well over six foot – and one was blond while the other was dark. They were just a few feet away. My eyes drank in the sight of their powerful, beefy backs. One of them – the dark-haired guy – turned to face me. He had rugged, handsome good looks, and I suddenly realised I was standing in the window dressed in a skimpy, baby-doll negligee. He grinned, lust written all over his face, and gave me the thumbs-up, while I pulled the curtains shut, mortified.

I got back into bed and picked up my magazine, trying to pretend I hadn't just 'flashed' at the gardeners, but the image of those two guys kept forcing its way into my mind. And with the image came the fantasy I'd had for years but had shut out (except at moments of wild orgasm, when it automatically kicked in and played in my head). The thought of two cocks inside me was my ultimate thrill. I imagined those two beefy guys coming into my room and fucking me as I screamed for more. They had to be strangers – that was all part of the fantasy. My clit began to throb and my hand left the magazine and crept under the duvet, searching for my warm, wet crack, but I stopped it.

Why didn't I make it happen? Those two guys were just a few feet away from my bedroom. Why masturbate over a fantasy when, if I played my cards right, it could happen for real?

I climbed out of bed, leaving a damp patch where my aching cunt had been, and opened the curtains before I had a chance to change my mind. Both guys were still lifting the heavy logs right near my window. I opened it and called out: 'Sorry. I didn't mean to expose myself. I just wondered if you'd like a coffee?'

The dark-haired guy walked over to the window. Close-up, I realised, he was stunningly handsome. His face was glistening with sweat.

'Thanks,' he replied, his eyes glancing at my tits in the fluffy pink negligee, which I'd carefully positioned so they were resting on the inside window ledge. We stood there in silence for a moment, drinking each other in, and the bulge in his trousers told me what I needed to know. I slid my middle finger sexily into my mouth and out again, then ran it down my neck and over my nipple. The bulge in his trousers grew even bigger. My eyes flicked down to his crotch and so did his. I licked my lips.

'Shall I come inside for it?' he asked, his voice barely a whisper. 'The coffee?'

I nodded. 'Flat 3, on the buzzer. But make sure you

bring your friend.'

I've never seen anyone look so shocked – or so thrilled. Best of all, I felt totally powerful and in control. I couldn't believe how assertive I was. But this was my fantasy and I was going to make it happen. Sex with Cassie had opened up a whole new world of possibilities and I was determined to enjoy them. His cock was clearly ready to burst out of his trousers, and a tiny wet patch told me that some pre-cum had leaked out of it, too.

He said something to his friend, who looked over at me, equally surprised, and the two of them practically ran to the front entrance. The buzzer sounded, sending a thrill right through me. I pressed the intercom to let them in, without a word.

'Bedroom's through here,' I called, as they made their way down the corridor.

'I'm Liam,' the dark-haired guy said, his hands visibly trembling. 'This is Jon.'

'You don't need to know my name,' I replied, laying back on the duvet and spreading my legs, exposing my bare, pink cunt. Liam took off his T-shirt and jeans, revealing a bronzed, hairy body and Jon, who seemed even more nervous, copied him. He was paler and hairless, but equally gorgeous. My eyes feasted on their dicks, Liam's tall, straight and thick, emerging magnificently from his dark pubic hair, while Jon's was smaller, more curved and surrounded by a pale blond bush. I knew exactly what I wanted – Liam in my cunt and Jon in my arse. They didn't look at each other's bodies – out of embarrassment, I guessed – but kept their gaze locked on my tits and cunt. Liam took the lead, lying down on one side of me while Jon copied him and lay down on the other. They smelled of damp earth and sweat, their hands covered in mud which turned to brown streaks on my moist skin as they stroked and kissed me. I grasped a cock in each hand and wanked them hard but slow, loving the feel of two gorgeous cocks and aching for the moment when they would both be inside me. Liam's hands were on my breasts, pulling me towards him, so I turned to face him. He took each tit in his mouth in turn, gently biting at my nipples which were hard as diamonds. Behind me, I could hear Jon masturbating fast, his breath coming in gasps as his other hand massaged my tits, his dirty fingers being sucked clean by Liam's huge mouth.

'Fuck me, both of you,' I breathed, and Liam plunged his cock into my pussy, the base pressed hard against my clit. Behind me, Jon continued wanking, and I realised he thought they were going to take it in turns, and I worried that he was going to come before he'd fucked me. I forced my arse backwards, with Liam still inside me, so that for a moment I had to lose the feeling of the base of his cock but I knew it would be worth it. My arsehole was rammed against the side of Jon's cock, his hand moving up and down the shaft like lightning. I took hold of his hand, held it still and eased his cock into my arse, so the head was just inside. 'Now fuck me, both of you,' I commanded, and after a moment of pain as Jon thrust his dick into me, I was overcome with the feeling of being properly fucked, properly full, for the first time in my life. Liam was fucking me harder than I'd ever been fucked, while Jon was gentler, trying to hold back his orgasm as long as possible. Suddenly Liam's whole body trembled and he shot his hot spunk deep into my cunt, his cock and Jon's rammed against each other inside me with just a thin barrier of flesh separating them. Jon let out a cry and tugged my nipples hard as his orgasm released his cum, and the feeling of those two, delicious cocks triggered my own, intense orgasm, rocking my whole body even harder than Cassie had done.

We lay together, entwined, until the boys finally withdrew. Each kissed me in turn and left without a word, huge grins on all our faces. It was more incredible than I can ever describe, and far better than my fantasy. I lay on the bed, thoroughly satisfied, with smears of mud still on my body and filled with their cum, feeling more alive than I'd ever dreamed possible. By the time I'd showered and dressed, the gardeners and their van had gone.

I sent Cassie a text to wish her well in the States, a

she replied saying simply, 'Thanks!' with three big kisses. Not many people can say this about their ex-boss, but because of her, I've given myself permission to enter a whole new sexual world – and I'm loving it.